EL DORADO TRAIL

The frontier of the early West stretched south for several hundred miles, down to Mexico, a country just recovering from the throes of revolution. The Civil War in the United States was finished, leaving both north and south impoverished. But along the southern trails there was silver to be had, dug out of the tall hills. Inevitably, the lawless breed drifted south. Cold, hard and vicious, they set up laws of their own, the law of the gun, and fought miner and Mexican alike in their lust for wealth.

BRETT CALDER

EL DORADO TRAIL

Complete and Unabridged

LINFORD
Leicester

First hardcover edition published in
Great Britain in 2002 by
Robert Hale Limited, London

Originally published in paperback as
'Danger Trail' by Chuck Adams

First Linford Edition
published 2004
by arrangement with
Robert Hale Limited, London

British Library CIP Data

Calder, Brett, *1928* –
   El Dorado trail.—Large print ed.—
Linford western library
1. Western stories 2. Large type books
I. Title II. Adams, Chuck. Danger trail
823.9'14 [F]

ISBN 1–84395–314–5

Published by
F. A. Thorpe (Publishing)
Anstey, Leicestershire

Set by Words & Graphics Ltd.
Anstey, Leicestershire
Printed and bound in Great Britain by
T. J. International Ltd., Padstow, Cornwall

This book is printed on acid-free paper

1

The Trail-Breakers

Crouched down against the rocks, Lanner cocked his rifle and pressed it close to his cheek as his red-rimmed eyes peered into the growing light of the steely dawn. His gaze moved restlessly ahead of him, searching for any sign of movement in the knife-edged shadows that clustered around him. He had heard the sound scant minutes before and in this barren, rock-strewn country to the south of the Texas border a man paused before he moved out in to the open, particularly at this time of the day, when he might be attacked without warning. Any untoward sound portended trouble and he had had several narrow shaves during the past two weeks as he had worked his way slowly south, across the desertlands and

1

through the hills that bordered them. The territory here was reputedly clear of Indians, but there had been smoke in the hills twenty miles to the north and he knew from what he had learned in Twin Buttes, the last town he had passed through on the trail, that this was also the favourite hunting ground of outlaws and killers, men who had deserted from the Army in the last months of the Civil War and had moved south into a new country where they forced a law all their own, the law of the sixgun.

Carefully, he scanned the battalion of shadows that lay in front of him. His horse was tethered to brush a little way back, wouldn't make a sound to betray him. The faint soughing of the wind, occasionally whipping up the red sand into stinging clouds of gritty particles that laced his mouth and eyes, made small sound in the grey half-light, sent little tremors of apprehension running up and down his spine. He lowered the rifle a little, rubbed with hard knuckles at his sore eyes. He had slept little that night, or the previous night. When moving through country like this, the haunt of men who would kill for a handful of gold, a man did not live long by taking chances. Straining his ears, he tried to pick out again the sound that had alerted him, but there was nothing. Had it been only his twisted imagination playing tricks with him? Desperately, he tried to separate fact from fantasy. There had been something there, he felt sure of it, and yet he could neither see nor hear anything.

Finally, tired of waiting, his leg muscles knotting themselves into painful cramp because of his strained position, he thrust the rifle out in front of him and edged out into the open, moving an inch at a time, eyes moved in his head, ready to lift the rifle and fire it at the slightest intimation of danger.

Still there was no sound of movement around him, but the fear came crowding back on him. More than ever before, he was certain now that there was someone there, probably with a rifle trained on the spot where he lay, just waiting for him to move further out into the open, so that he might draw a bead on him and send a slug into his body.

There were tricky overtones to the shadows that clustered more thickly to his right, where a number of narrow, though deep ravines cut through the hard rocky ground. For a moment, he paused on all fours, then the sound came, clearly this time, over to his right. Frayed nerves and fatigue made him jump and swing round sharply, bringing up the rifle, his finger hard on the trigger. When no bullet came to meet him, he moved forward once more, reached the lip of one of the narrow, steep-sided ravines and peered down, the barrel of the rifle thrust forward. Then he lowered it quickly to the rocks beside him, leaned further forward as he glimpsed the figure huddled at the bottom of the ravine. He could only just make out the grey blur of the man's face, streaked with dust and blood.

Bending, he reached down with one hand, saw the other peering up at him. Then the man extended his own hand and Lanner grabbed it, pulled. The other moaned again, tried to scrabble for a handhold with his legs, failed, and Lanner was forced to take his dead weight, dragging him up the steep side of the ravine until he had him stretched out on the ground close by. The man's breathing was harsh and his features pale under the beard. He tried to struggle to a sitting position, but sank back with a low gasp, one hand fluttering up to his chest. Lanner saw the ugly stain of blood there, ripped the shirt back. The slug had gone in deep, just below the breastbone and there was no sign of it having come out at the back.

'God, but it burns inside,' murmured the other harshly.

'Just lie still and I'll get you some water.' Getting to his feet, he went back to where his mount was tethered, took down the canteen and returned to where the man lay on his back close to the ravine. Propping up the other's head, he held the lip of the canteen to the other's mouth, let him sip the cold water slowly. A drink was no good to a man as badly hurt as this man, but Lanner guessed that it would make no difference now. There was the indelible shadow of death clear to see in his expression; in the dark-circled and unnaturally bright and motionless eyes.

Drinking a little, the stranger suddenly turned his head away from the canteen. 'Thanks, mister,' he said in a low tone, so that his words were scarcely audible. 'It don't burn so bad now.'

'Who shot you?' Lanner asked tersely. He sat back on his haunches, still holding the canteen in has fingers.

'Never saw their faces. More'n one of 'em. Reckon there must've been a whole bunch. Bushwhacked me in the rocks, shot me down and took my horse, rolled me into the ravine and left me for dead.' He took in a gulp of air. 'Reckon they weren't far wrong at that.' His lips twisted into a tight grimace as a spasm of agony lanced through his body, arching it from the rocks. Then, exhausted by the effort, he fell back and lay so still that for a moment, Lanner felt sure that he was dead.

Then he murmured softly: 'That slug, it went all the way in?'

'Reckon so,' Lanner nodded. 'From front to back below the breastbone.'

'I figured that,' he gave a slow nod. 'I heard you ridin' over the ledge yonder and tried to yell, but I wasn't certain you'd heard me.'

'I heard somethin'. Wasn't sure what it was. Nearly shot you down there.'

'This place is full of snakes,' affirmed the other. His fading gaze fixed itself on the man who knelt over him. 'Can't see you too well now, stranger. Seems to be gettin' dark all of a sudden.'

Lanner glanced up, saw that the dawn was brightening swiftly now over to the east, a wide grey strip of sky lying over the horizon. Pretty soon, the sun would come up, glaring and hot.

The other sighed and his breath came rattling out of his throat. 'You want to know why they shot me down from ambush, mister?'

Lanner let his gaze travel back to the other's pain-twisted features. Up until that moment he had scarcely paused to consider that. Such events as this were common enough in this territory, this lawless and utterly untamed land.

'They probably figured you'd got somethin' valuable in your saddle bags,' he answered.

'Valuable, yeah.' The other nodded his head with an obvious effort. 'But it weren't in the saddle bag. Only a fool would carry anythin' in there. First place these *hombres* look.' He lifted one arm wearily, as if the effort was too much for him, pointed a hand in the direction of his leg. 'In the boot there,' he said harshly. 'It's yours, stranger. I won't be needin' anythin' like that where I'm headed. This is one trail where I can take nothin' with me.'

Reaching down, Lanner pulled off the other's boot. At first, he could see nothing, then upturning the boot, he saw something fall out, hit the rocks with a dull thud. Picking it up, he turned it over in his hand, saw the bright glint of the dawn light on it.

'It's silver, all right,' murmured the man hoarsely. 'Plenty more where that came from. Those *hombres* must've been lookin' for that when they jumped me. That — and the . . . ' His voice trailed off into a harsh bout of coughing and there were tiny specks of blood on his lips, his face drained of all colour, a bloodless mask with the dark circles standing out under the deep-sunk eyes.

Lanner picked up the canteen, held it out again, but the other shook his head with his last remaining strength.

'Save it,' he said croakingly, somehow getting the words out. 'You'll need every last drop of water to cross that country ahead, before you hit the main silver trail. No sense wastin' it on a dyin' man.'

Glancing up, Lanner stared out across the barren country which surrounded them, grey and pale in the dawn light. A harsh, cruel and relentless land which would not yield to man. He pushed the cork back into the canteen, heard the faint, steady *slop* of the water inside. Somewhere in the rocks, he heard the soft slithering motion of a lizard.

Then, closer at hand, he heard a slight sigh that came from the dying man, saw the softness that came to his limbs and muscles, the way his features seemed to loosen, smoothing away all of the lines of fear and pain. It was almost as if he had slipped into sleep. Gently, Lanner touched the other with a probing hand, knew that life was no longer there. He stood up, staring down at the other, then at the silver nugget in his hand. Thrusting it into his pocket, he bent to close the wide, staring eyes and as he did so, caught sight of something white inside the boot from which the nugget had dropped. Pulling it out, he turned the tattered piece of paper over in his hands for a moment before opening it, holding it up to the light.

For several moments, the lines and figures marked on it failed to make any sense to him. Then he realized that it was a map, a rough drawing it was true, but one which gave him sufficient details to discover the location of the spot which was marked in rough pencil 'Silver found here'.

Slowly, he folded it, thrust it into his pocket together with the silver nugget. It was evident that the other had made this silver strike somewhere to the south of the desert here, had perhaps been on his way back there when he had been dry-gulched and killed. But his attackers had not found the silver or the map.

'I guess they didn't get very much after shootin' you down,' he said to the corpse. He took one quick look about him, then fell to work scooping out a shallow grave in the sandy soil among the rocks. Afterwards, he piled large stones and boulders over the grave to keep out marauding beasts that might otherwise come to dig up the dead man. Funny, he reflected, as he made his way back to his mount, still standing patiently among the tall, upthrusting boulders, but he did not even know the name of the man he had buried. Just another nameless wanderer in this wild and terrible land, a man who had died by violence and now lay buried in an unmarked grave, miles from anywhere.

He swung up into the saddle, rode past the pile of stones, reined up for a moment looking down at them, then touched spurs to his horse's flanks and rode on into the brightening redness of a new day on the trail. The sun lifted, grew warm and then almost unbearably hot. He rode listlessly, without spirit. There had been, a while earlier that morning, a pang of hunger gnawing at his belly, but it was gone now and there was just a strange emptiness, no feeling at all in him. All he wanted to do now was ride along with his mount, letting it drift along at its own pace, not having to direct his horse or even to think, to remember. It was odd how that unknown man's death could have such an effect on him. Men died quickly here, either in fair or unfair fight, lives were cheap and the old ways of violence unchanging. He began to ponder on the map he had found. Was it genuine, or had the other merely thought he had found a rich strike? Certainly the fact that he had been carrying the large nugget of silver with him pointed to the fact that he must have known of some rich strike somewhere and the directions on the crudely drawn map were such that a man might follow them reasonably easily.

Tired from such futile wondering, he pulled the canteen from its holder, tilted it to his lips and drank sparingly on the water, letting it slide slowly down his throat, slaking his thirst a little although there was a deep parched dryness within him and he felt like a board, left out far too long in the hot sun, left until it was warped and withered.

Throughout the day, he had kept his eyes open for some sign of the trail which should have been left by those killers who had shot down the old man, but he had seen nothing. He guessed they had either ridden north, or had cut back on their own trail, making it virtually impossible to follow them.

The country through which he rode was new to him, but he felt no concern. The long, bitter, violent years during the war, the battle in the Wilderness where men had died on either side of him and he had been unable to save them, had forged something deep and strong within him, something that could not be broken. He was a part of this great country now. He had fought for it and in the steel of battle, he had become tempered. He rode through the narrow cut of a dry creek, saw the sun almost touch the skyline far to the west, knew it would soon be dark and he would have to make another camp in the open. He led his mount up the slope and found stunted pine at the top. Beyond them, as far as the eye could see, stretched a barren and inhospitable land, open country that was cut off here and there by rocky upthrusts. There was a sudden rise of birds from among the trees at his approach but no further alien sound. He stopped among the trees to listen and then satisfied himself there was no danger there.

He made a cold camp, not wishing to light a fire for fear of being seen and in addition, his grub was getting low. He had shot a small deer two days before, but the food was almost gone.

In the morning, he examined the map once more, studying it closely. Had that old fellow made this map? he wondered; or had it been made by someone else and been given to him? It was probably a question that would never be answered. Folding it, he pushed it back into his pocket, rolled himself a smoke, felt it bring some of the warmth back into his chest, for the night had been bitterly cold with a searching wind blowing off the mesa, cutting through the trees and the thin undergrowth, freezing him to the marrow.

He rode hard most of the morning and by high noon crossed a river at a ford where the bottom sands were scarcely covered by water, two inches perhaps, that splashed a little around his horse's hoofs as it picked its way to the other side. He made noon camp in the shade of a small cluster of trees growing out of the river bank, his hat pulled well down over his face to shield him from the heat and the glinting light of the sun that shone through the branches over his head. The heat was a terrible burning pressure now, all about him, so that there was no respite from it. In the shade of the trees one could get away from the harsh glare of the sunlight, but the heat was reflected from the rocks and the river, rolling back from the punished earth in shimmering waves that brought the sweat pouring from his limbs and made a thin, scarcely seen turbulence in the atmosphere around him. There was the hard smell of burnt grass and sage hanging in the air, mingling with the bitter dust. His face was a mask of yellow where the dust had worked its way into the folds of the skin, mixing with the sweat, caking on his cheeks. Stretched out on his back he clasped his hands behind his neck, stared up at the patches of pale blue sky over him, sky that seemed to have been dull-washed of all colour by the blistering of the sun, set like a distant furnace in the heavens. In the spotty shade of the tree, he finally fell asleep, did not waken until the sunlight lanced on his upturned face, glaring redly even through the closed lids. He rubbed the dust on his face where it was burning and scorching him, found that only made the discomfort worse and got to his feet, going down to the river where it ran a little more deeply and strongly than at the ford. Lying flat on his belly he thrust his head under the cool water, felt the mask of dust pop on his face as it melted away. The cool water stung his flesh but he felt better as he lifted his head, shaking the sparkling drops from his hair. He brought the horse forward and let it drink, slowly and not too much. They had still a long distance to cover and both man and beast were better not to sweat too much. To ride dry was easier on both of them.

When he finally stepped into the saddle, he turned south once more, in the direction he had been travelling for more than thirty days now, always south, down to the Rio Grande and beyond. He sat tall and limber in the saddle, a man bred to this kind of life, face burned the colour of old leather by long years of exposure to the strong sunlight, eyes a keen grey under the lower brows, a rider's looseness about him, features and shape solid and flat.

Looking back over his shoulder, he

half expected to see the shadow of a dust cloud on that flat, rolling country which lay behind him. But there was nothing there but the heat-shimmering flatness and a horizon that trembled and swayed at the back of the glare. The man he had found the previous day was the only one he had seen during the whole of his time on the trail. He had deliberately shunned most of the towns he had reached, preferring his own company to that of any of the Northern carpetbaggers who were systematically ruining the south now that it had been defeated.

Midway through the long, heat-filled afternoon, he sighted a ranch headquarters on the horizon, a low cluster of buildings that stood out against the flat, rolling plain. He made a wide sweep to line himself up to the ranch. It was not that he felt in need of any company even now after so long alone on the trail, but it was possible he might get food there and there was no way of telling how much further he would have to travel before he reached the next sign of human habitation. In another hour, he was close enough to make out the buildings clearly. The middle-down sun burned them a harsh colour, but from that distance he saw no sign of life there. Curious, he slowed his mount, reined up at the top of a slight rise that overlooked the ranch. In the distance, on the upgrade slope of a low hill, he saw a small herd of stringy cattle. There was a couple of horses in the corral in front of the main building with a small barn and a bunkhouse nearby. Knitting his brows a little in thoughtful concentration, he sat easily in the saddle, rolled a smoke and kept a thoughtful eye on the place for several minutes, watching for any sign of movement. The sun was hot on his back and shoulders and the smoke dried his mouth, giving him little pleasure. When there was no movement from the ranch after he had finished his smoke, he rode through the ankle-deep grass, dry and brown in the harsh sunlight. When he got nearer, he saw that the ranch door was open and as he rode into the dry, dusty courtyard, a man stepped out, a man with an ancient rifle held in his hands, the barrel pointed at Lanner.

'All right, mister,' he called hoarsely. 'That's far enough. Now jest turn around and ride on out of here.'

'Hold on there,' Lanner said quietly. He rested his elbows on the pommel of the saddle, leaning forward a little and studying the other closely. 'I don't mean any harm. Just want to buy a little grub, that's all. I'll pay for anythin' I get.'

The other seemed to consider that for a moment, but the barrel of the rifle never wavered in the rock-steady hands. Then the rancher smiled in a wintry sort of way. 'I've heard of your kind before,' he said thinly. 'Any more like you hidin' up yonder in the trees, waitin' to ride in?'

Lanner shook his head slowly, wearily. 'I'm ridin' light,' he answered. 'And there's nobody with me.' From that distance, he noticed the look of strain, and perhaps fear, on the other's lined, weatherbeaten face. Meanwhile, he waited for the other to consider his offer to buy food. The man's decision seemed to be a long time in coming. Then another voice spoke up from the doorway at the back of the rancher.

'He doesn't look like the others. I think he can be trusted.' A girl stepped out into the open, tall and slender, eyes regarding Lanner with a half-amused stare.

The rancher paused and seemed to speculate on him further, then he nodded and lowered the rifle reluctantly. 'All right, get down man and put your horse into the corral. It'll be safe there.'

Lanner dismounted, led his horse through the wooden gate in the circular fence and then walked back towards the house, his mouth felt dry and his legs were stiff from the long hours spent in the saddle. There was a trough and a water pipe in front of the house and he bent and drank his fill, then straightened and walked over to the two standing in front of the doorway.

'Thanks,' he said quietly. 'It's dry work ridin' in that sun.'

'You look as though you've ridden a long way,' said the girl. She gave him a faint and uncertain smile, running her gaze over him. 'My name is Rosalia Winton and this is my father, Jethroe.'

'Clint Lanner.' said the other, introducing himself. He nodded. 'I've been ridin' for nearly thirty days now, heading south all the time. There seem to be mighty few places in this territory where a man can buy grub.'

'You're welcome to what little we have here,' said Jethroe Winton. He placed the ancient Sharps against the side of the porch. 'Better get in out of the sun.'

Thankfully, Lanner stepped on to the wide porch. The air was a little cooler here but the glare from the dusty courtyard still glanced painfully in his eyes whenever he turned to stare out into the distance, levelling his gaze on the low hills.

'You jest ridin' through?' asked Winton, his eyes wide open and watching him keenly and sharply. 'You seem pretty much on the jump. Ain't nobody chasing you, are there?'

Lanner shook his head. 'From the way you acted back there, I figure you've met up with men who want more'n grub.'

'This is a bad country,' the girl said, her voice quiet, but with a little edge of strain to it. 'We're tolerated here because we mind our own business. But further to the south there are the outlaw bands who rob the miners and the Mexicans alike.'

'Miners?' queried Lanner, looking over at her.

'Silver,' said Winton roughly. 'There is plenty to be had in the hills, fifty or sixty miles from here but the outlaws and killers have moved in. There isn't a week goes by without somebody being jumped and killed.'

24

'And the law does nothin' about it?'

'The law.' There was a scornful note in the girl's voice. She moved towards the kitchen at the back of the house. 'There's no law here except that which the outlaws bring with them. Some of the miners tried to band together to defeat these killers, but after a dozen or so of them were shot down, they gave up the idea.'

After she had gone into the kitchen, and Lanner heard her working with the pans and dishes, the older man, standing in the doorway, resting his shoulders against the wall, said earnestly. 'You see now why we have to be careful whenever anybody rides up to the ranch. What few cattle I have here, I aim to keep. But it wouldn't be easy if these *hombres* decided they wanted my beef for themselves. They've burned a lot of small ranches, killed the owners or forced them out of the territory.'

Lanner remembered the dying man he had met up with on the trail, knew what lay behind this man's words. It

25

was a common enough occurrence in these frontier territories. Before law and order moved in, there had to be this period of lawlessness when the bitter stench of gunsmoke lay over the prairies and men died with a surprising suddenness. These people were eking out a precarious existence here, living from one day to the next, not knowing when their turn would come to face the sixguns of the outlaws.

The girl came back with some dishes, set them on the table. From the kitchen there came the appetizing aroma of frying beef and potatoes, stinging the inside of his jaws, making him realize how long it was since he had eaten anything like this. When the meal was ready, he lowered himself gratefully into the chair at the table, then ate hungrily, sitting back with all of his muscles loose, fully enjoying the laziness and the luxury of the meal. He was aware of their eyes on him as he ate, knew they were still wondering about him. They had probably already decided he was no outlaw and probably guessed that he was not a fugitive on the run from the law; but it was unusual for a man to come riding these trails unless he had something in mind and they were anxious to know what it might be, although he knew they would keep their questions until he had eaten.

At last, he pushed the clean plate from him, sipped the hot coffee that had been placed at his elbow. The food had acted as a stimulant to him and he built himself a cigarette, offering the meagre pouch to the other. He smiled a little, drawing his brows together so that shrewd lines appeared on his forehead and above the bridge of his nose.

'I'm obliged to you for your kindness,' he said at length.

'Glad to have you here,' nodded Winton. 'You headed for the silver mines?'

'Hadn't really thought about it' he confessed openly. 'Since the war finished, I've been wanderin', not findin' any place to settle down. Figured that if

I headed south, there might be some job I could find here where there's nobody tryin' to grab off everythin' for themselves. Up north, even in Texas, men are starvin' while there's a market waitin' for their beef. They've got an empire there of a million square miles and more cattle than you can count, but they're bein' forced to trade steers for sacks of flour to eat. That was no place for me, I had to get away. Fiddle-footed, I guess.'

'A man could do worse than that, I reckon,' answered the other. 'But whether you'll find anythin' better to the south than what you left behind in Texas, I don't know. There are men there with the habits of coyotes!'

'You figure they may pay you a visit sometime in the future?' asked Lanner sharply.

Winton hesitated. He looked uncomfortable. 'You might say that. They're treacherous and you never know where they mean to strike next.'

'Do you mean to keep on riding

south, or will you be staying awhile in these parts?' asked the girl.

Lanner appeared to deliberate. He finished his coffee, nodded as the girl held out the jug again. 'I might hang around here for a spell,' he said finally, studying her face.

'And you might ride on?'

'Sure. Depends on what I find in this neck of the woods. You heard of a place called the Silver Trail?'

Winton eyed him, eyes suddenly narrowed. Then he gave a slow nod of his head. 'Sure, who hasn't?' He got to his feet and walked to the window. 'It's about thirty miles south of here, used to be part of the frontier between Texas and Mexico. That's the trail most of the silver is taken along after it's been mined from the hills. That's where you'll find most of these outlaw bands.' He hesitated, then said tautly. 'You look like a decent enough young fella to me. Moving out there is none of your business. Better keep away from those parts or you're likely to regret it.

There's an extra place here if you've got no other place to go in a hurry and you're welcome to stick around for a while.'

'Thanks. Reckon I'm in no big hurry, I guess I could stick around for a couple of days.' Lanner felt a faint cold chill in him, but did not allow it to show through on to his face. There was no knowing to what lengths this man would go to protect his ranch from these killers. He might even go to the length of trying to keep him here as a hired hand, in the belief that three guns were better than two if it came to a showdown with the outlaws.

★　★　★

Lanner stayed at the small ranch for three days. During the whole of that time, he saw no one other than Winton and his daughter, although on two occasions when riding the perimeter of the spread, he had glimpsed the dust-smoke in the distance that told of other riders in the neighbourhood, but they were many miles distant, curving away from the ranch, so far away that it was impossible even to pick out the sound of hoofbeats. Yet for some off-hand reason, the mere sight of them stirred a faint, but growing, apprehension in his mind. He thought more and more of that map and the silver nugget in his pocket, wondered about them. Perhaps there was a rich silver mine there at the spot marked on the scrap of paper. And if that was the case, then he was entitled to it. The dying man had given it to him of his own free will and that meant the mine was, perhaps, legally his if he ever managed to locate it.

On the fourth morning, he saddled his mount before sun-up, tightening the cinch under the animal's belly, as the ranch door opened and the girl came out. She caught sight of him instantly, and came over, a curiously indrawn expression on her clear-cut, regular features. She said: 'Are you pulling out?'

'That's right. I figure I've overstayed my welcome here and besides, there's a little unfinished business I have to attend to. Maybe, when it's finished, I'll ride back.'

'If we're still here,' said the girl seriously. Her eyes were troubled.

'You mean if the outlaws come?' he queried sharply.

For a moment, she did not answer. Then she gave a quick nod of the head. 'I'm afraid they may. I thought that as long as you were here, we were a little safer.'

'But your father says that so far, they've never bothered you. I reckon that if they meant to attack you, or run your beef off, they'd have done it long ago.'

Concern crept into her eyes, only now it was tempered by fear. 'There are men moving south all the time, lured here by the prospect of getting rich in the shortest possible time. They're hungry by the time they reach here and are on the look-out for food. They'll take all they can lay their hands on, and if we tried to stop them, they'd kill us.' She tried desperately to keep the quiver out of her voice.

'You really think that will happen?'

'I — oh, I don't know.' She spoke through tight lips. 'I keep feeling that we've stayed here too long already. I've tried to talk my father into selling the place and pulling out, going back to Texas. But he won't hear of it. He's a man with a lot of pride and he says that no outlaws are going to run him off his own land, that he'll fight them with everything he has if they try.'

'Can't you make him see that it's no use tryin' to fight these men if they mean business? Better to pull out with a whole skin and a little money than finish up here six feet under the ground, all for the sake of a little stiff-necked pride.'

She was silent for a long moment after that. Then quietly, she went on: 'Are you sure you won't be able to stay for a little while? At least until I've had another talk with him, tried to make him see sense.'

'I'd like to, Miss Winton. Believe me, I would. But it just ain't possible.' He twisted his lips into a lop-sided grin. He saw the girl's set face. Then she swung abruptly away and went back into the ranch.

For a moment, he watched her as she walked up on to the porch, then vanished into the house. Certainly this country was no place for a girl like that, he told himself, busying himself with the horse. Why her father was such a stubborn old cuss, he did not know. Going inside a few moments later, he heard her in the kitchen. There was the smell of cooking in the air and Winton, standing over by the window looking out over the flat, dusty courtyard said quietly: 'See you're saddling up your mount, Clint. Sorry you can't stay around longer, but I quite see your point. If a man has business to attend to, he's better to get it over and done with first, before he starts anythin' else.'

Breakfast was a meal of silences, quickly over. Lanner was aware of the girl watching him at intervals from beneath lowered lids. When it was finished, Lanner went out on to the porch and a moment later, Winton came out and stood beside him.

'I hope you realize the sort of trouble you'll be ridin' into, Clint,' he said slowly, carefully. 'This is bad country, no law and order here and not likely to be any in our lifetimes.' His mouth thinned into a tight line. 'I saw Rosalia talkin' with you earlier. Reckon she was askin' you to stay around for a while longer.'

'That's right,' Clint nodded. 'She seems to think that you're maybe in more danger than I am. Seems to me you'd be better selling up this place for what you can get for it, and moving back north. No place for a girl.'

'You reckon I haven't thought about that before now!' There was a harsh note to the other's tone. He straightened up. 'Everythin' I have I put into this place. There was nothin' here but empty, bare desert when I came out here more'n fifteen years ago. Now, at least, I've built somethin' here with my bare hands and it's all mine. I don't give up a thing like that very easily and I'll fight for what is mine. If ever this country is to become big, then it needs someplace like this, and more besides, bigger and better ranches. This country will grow corn and beef if only it's given the chance.'

'Those outlaws don't seem to think so.'

'That's true. Nothin' we can do about them until we get some law here.'

'The Government won't do anythin' for you. This is no-man's-land as far as they are concerned. Both America and Mexico lay claims to this stretch of land and until they've made up their minds about it one way or the other, they won't care overmuch about giving you any protection from these killers. But what about the other homesteaders? There must be plenty like you around here, more so to the south, I reckon. Why don't you band together and form some sort of front against these outlaws?'

'And start a range war down here like those they had in Texas a few years ago? How long do you think that would last and who do you reckon would win it even if most of the others would throw in their lot with us?'

Lanner had no answer for that, knew instinctively that the other was speaking plain sense. He remembered a little of the range wars that had flared up at frequent intervals in Texas. Bad days when the range had been turned into a blazing hell and more men had been killed than he could count. He could understand these people here not wanting the same sort of thing to happen along the Rio Grande.

He cast a quick glance at the sun, now lifting over the swaying tops of the trees on the hill. It was time to be moving out. Stepping down from the porch into the courtyard, he paused and turned, holding out his hand. 'Thanks again for your hospitality,' he said. 'I'll look out for you if I ride back this way.'

'I'll be here,' said the other confidently. He gave a little nod as he released the other's hand.

He walked slowly to the waiting horse, swung up into the saddle, holding the reins loosely in his hands. The heat of the day had not yet risen and there was a refreshing coolness in the air at the moment. But there were a few eddies of dust lifting in the distance to the south, giving a hint of what was to come.

He was on the point of moving out, when the girl came out on to the porch, saw him and came forward slowly. Her face still bore that troubled look he had seen earlier.

'I can't change my mind,' he said tightly, speaking through his teeth. 'But I will head back this way, I promise.'

'I hope you will,' she said in a low voice. 'But be careful. If you feel you have to go south, then nothing will stop you.'

'I'll take care,' he said softly. He gave the horse a soft touch of the spurs, headed out of the courtyard and took the narrow, winding trail over the low hill. The sun was up now, climbing swiftly into a cloudless sky. Tiny dust devils lifted around him as he went downgrade. Further along, he discovered a rock-flanked trail which soon led him to a place where he could climb to the head of the buttes, so that he was able to look down over the vast plain which lay spread before him, out to the limitless horizons. Reaching the open range, he gave the horse its head, anxious to get to the far side of this range. He did not like these open spaces where a man could ride for a day, two days, and get nowhere. But when a man had long distances to cover, the best way was often the easy way. He sat tall and easy in the saddle for his own comfort and also to save the horse. He rode the many miles in steady silence. The stillness that pressed in with the heat from the horizons was such that it made a man conscious of his utter smallness and especially at night, with the stars shining so brilliantly in the yeasty ferment of the universe, so low it seemed he had only to reach up to brush them with his little finger. It was as if a man could hear the voice of God speaking out across the vast, tremendous wilderness.

On the second day after leaving the Winton ranch, he made his way slowly through the long canyon with the sheer rocky walls lifting almost a hundred feet on either side of him. He had spotted signs of many men around him, but had been unable to tell whether they were Indian or white. Because of this, he had travelled more slowly during the long afternoon, more cautiously. He did not want to run into trouble with his eyes shut.

2

Wild Town

The town, when he finally reached it, late that evening, was a sprawling place that lay on both sides of the broad, sandy trail running due north and south. It consisted mainly of rough wooden structures which, away from the main street, fronted on to narrow, twisting alleys, rubbish-filled, swarming with tiny flies. In the centre of the town, the street widened still further, became a dusty place where tall cottonwoods broke the drabness and provided shade in the heat of midday. The few people on the street, mostly Mexicans, but with a sprinkling of Americans, eyed him without much curiosity. There were too many of his kind riding through these small frontier towns.

When he came to the livery, he

handed his horse to the tiny, barefoot Mexican boy, then made for the cantina. It was cool inside the long, low-roofed building. There was a small group of men standing at the long bar and he noticed how their eyes flickered in his direction, watching him closely although appearing not to see him. He went across to the bar, stood with his elbows on it, not taking any interest in the other men. They had looked a hard-faced crew, men with the dust of the trail still on them. He reckoned there might be some cattle outfits close by this place. It had looked to be a typical cow-town when he had ridden in, probably one of the first stops for any gangs rustling beef across the border.

The bartender came forward, a short, fat Mexican. He stopped in front of Clint, eyed him up and down for a moment, then said with a flash of white teeth: 'What will it be *señor*?'

'Whisky or beer,' Clint said, 'anythin' so long as it's cool and wet.'

'Sure.' The other nodded, went back along the bar and came back with a bottle and glass which he set down in front of him. Clint poured himself a glass of the whisky, downed it in a single gulp. It burned the back of his throat, but washed the trail dust from his mouth and brought an expanding haze of warmth into his stomach.

'You a stranger in this town, mister?'

Clint turned slowly as the harsh voice called to him from the other end of the bar. One of the group of men was staring at him closely, narrowed eyes set close against a thick nose, a red moustache drooping on either side of the broad lips.

'Just rode in,' said Clint carefully. 'First place of this size I've seen since I started out some time ago.'

'Lookin' for anythin' in particular, or just ridin' through?' The way the man said it left no doubt that he hoped the latter was the course Clint proposed to take.

'Depends.' Clint poured a second

43

glass, sipped it slowly, eyeing the other over the rim. 'Might be I'll stick around for a little while.'

'Might be that could be dangerous.' The other's voice was edged with menace.

'Could be I'm used to it.' Clint did not look at the other as he spoke, but his mouth felt suddenly dry and the small hairs on the nape of his neck began to tingle a little. He knew it was the wrong answer when he spoke, saw the other's slitted mouth as he pushed himself away from the bar.

'Mister,' said the moustached one hoarsely. 'We don't take kindly to strangers ridin' into town unless we know why they're here.'

Clint raised his brows, noticing that the other had stepped from the bar so that he had freedom to move his right hand. 'If you're meanin' why have I come here, that's my business.' His tone hardened just a shade as he went on. 'I'm a peaceable man if folk let me stay that way but I can bite as well as the next man if anybody starts a-pushing.'

The bartender said sharply. 'No shooting in here, *señors*. He means nothing Red. I theenk when he knows — '

'He knows enough now,' roared the man called Red. He watched Clint in the same way a snake watches a rabbit, through unblinking eyes, like polished pebbles in his head, waiting for the right moment to make his play. 'Reckon you've got to be taught a lesson, Mister. Nobody comes in here bucking us.'

Clint gave no sign of noticing the harshness in the other's tone. He finished the whisky in his glass, rubbed his mouth with the back of his hand. This was not the first time he had found himself in a dangerous and precarious position such as this. He knew these men for the kind they were, cruel and vicious killers, believing that they ran this town, that they were the law here and everyone else either conformed to it, or they called them out, shooting them down. These men were all ripe for trouble, were wanting to meet it more than halfway. He caught a glimpse out of the corner of his eye of the sneering smile on a short, stubby man's face, standing just behind the red-haired man. The stubby man nudged the other, said something in his ear, then stepped abruptly away from the bar, moving towards the middle of the room. Clint guessed the reason behind the move at once. As soon as Red made his play, the other man would draw too, hoping to take him from two sides. It was an old trick. The rest of the men would stay out of the play so as not to interfere with their two companions.

The bartender said something more in a high, squeaky voice, made a move to duck down behind the counter, then froze as one of the men in the background snapped. 'Just remain where you are, Miguel. We'll have none of these shotgun tactics here. This is a personal fight.'

The bartender stepped back, placed

his hands flat on the top of the counter, his face shaking a little with fear, trying not to let it show through. He swallowed thickly, eyes bulging in his head.

Clint's cold gaze flickered back to the red-headed man. He smiled thinly. He said slowly. 'You don't seem very sure of this, Red. Seems to me you've got to have your friend standing by to back up your play. That how you keep the law in this cow-town?'

Hate came into the other's face. It showed in the set of his mouth and the bulging of the muscles of his jaw and cheeks. He didn't like that veiled jibe, although Clint knew that it would make no difference to the way things were going to go here. These men had made up their minds that he represented some sort of menace and they were determined to eliminate him.

The man's features worked under the swarthy skin and there was a faint filming of sweat showing on his forehead, with little beads trickling down the side of his face. He let his right hand hang low over the butt of his sagging pistol. 'Get away from that bar,' he said a moment later in a rasping tone.

Clint set down his empty glass. He was aware of the bartender eyeing him with a curious expression on his face, evidently trying to gauge what sort of man this was who was standing up to these men, knowing their reputation.

He moved away from the bar slowly and now his eyes were unfocused so that he was able to watch both men at once so that the slightest movement would be seen. The man with the drooping moustache stood in a half-stance, his hot gaze fixed on Clint and for the first time, the outlaw did not look quite as sure of himself as he had before. Was it possible that he had misjudged this man who stood facing them? It was just possible that this man was a blood-thirsty killer, a gunslick with a reputation as a fast gun, who could shoot down all of them in a single instant of red-blasted time.

'You've made this play, Red.' Clint said softly, menacingly. He gave a smile of grim satisfaction. 'I reckon you'd like to back down now, you just made a bum play callin' me.'

'You reckon so, mister,' snarled the other tersely. His eyes glinted savagely and for just a moment his head moved in the direction of the other man standing a few feet from him. Almost as if it had been a pre-arranged signal, he made his play.

Red was fast, dangerously fast and even as his hand streaked down from the gun at his belt, he yelled harshly: *'Get him, Clem!'*

From the edge of his vision, Clint saw the other gunman going for his gun. Then in a blur that was far quicker than the eye could follow, his own guns were in his fists, seeming to leap into them of their own volition, his thumbs jerking back on the hammers and letting them slam down on the cartridges. Only Red got off one solitary shot, the slug ploughing into the floor in front of him as he swayed drunkenly under the smashing impact of the bullet. Clem died on his feet before his pistol had cleared leather, legs buckling weakly under him. He fell sideways, giving the table near him a sideswipe with one arm that sent it flying as he went down.

Red stood upright for a long moment, a look of shocked, stunned disbelief on his face as he fought desperately to hold life in the glazing eyes that stared at Clint, straining to put some last ounce of strength into his hand to realign the barrel of his Colt on Clint's chest. But the strength and the life were ebbing out of his body fast. His left hand clawed momentarily for the bar as he strove to keep himself on his feet. Then he pitched forward, his gun dropping from his lifeless fingers. In that frozen second, Clint's voice lashed at the other men standing in the background in a loose bunch.

'Don't any of you try to go for your

guns!' he snapped. His own pistols covered them, preventing any such move, although it was not strictly necessary. From their expressions it was clear that none of the men there had even considered it possible for this to be the outcome of the fight. They had expected him to die under the guns of one of the men.

Out of the corner of his vision, he saw the swarthy bartender wipe sweat from his face with the back of his hand. Slowly, the look of amazement faded from the Mexican's features.

Clint let his gaze wander over the faces of the men standing at the bar. He said gratingly: 'I figure you'd better get out of here and ride. If I see any of your faces again, I'll come gunnin' for you.'

The men eyed him sullenly, then moved away as one man from the bar, out through the doors of the cantina and into the dusty street. Clint stood in the open doorway, watched as they swung up into the saddle, two of them gripping the reins of the horses which had belonged to Red and Clem. One of the men leaned down and said through thinned lips. 'You reckon you've won this round, stranger. But it won't be long before we come ridin' into town lookin' for you. And if we find you still here, things are goin' to go bad for you!' There was the promise of death in his voice. Then he wheeled his mount and rode off with the rest following close behind, taking the trail that led to the south of the town. The dust cloud lifted and clung to the air, shimmering in the sunlight. Not until they had swung out of sight at the end of the main street did Clint thrust the guns back into their holsters and step back into the cantina.

Pouring himself another drink at the bar, he said casually: 'You know any of those *hombres*, bartender?'

'Sure, sure,' said the other quickly. His teeth flashed whitely in his head. 'They are a bad bunch of men, all of them.' He rubbed at the top of the counter with a damp cloth. 'But I reckon you showed them who was the best man here.'

'Who are they?' he asked pointedly. It seemed strange they should have picked a fight with him like that. He could not recall having seen any of them before and yet there must have been a reason why they should have tried to kill him.

'Some of Durman's coyboys, *señor*.'

'Durman? Who's he?' queried Clint softly.

'A beeg man in thees territory. Has many head of cattle. His ranch lies across the trail south of here, half a day's ride maybe.'

'Is he the law in these parts then?'

The other shrugged. 'There ees a Sheriff in town, *señor*, and he weel hear of this and want to question you.'

Scarcely had the other spoken than the doors swung open and a stout, bull-necked man strode in, the badge on his shirt pinned where everyone could see it. His eyes swivelled to take in everything. His gaze flickered over Clint and then fell on the two bodies stretched out in front of the bar. Going forward he went down on one knee, turned Red over, then sucked in a sharp, incredulous breath. There was a curious look on his face as he straightened up, eyeing Clint warily. 'All right,' he said with a touch of weariness to his tone, 'what happened here?'

Clint shrugged. 'Just what it looks like, Sheriff,' he said. 'These two *hombres* called me out and drew on me first.'

For an instant, there was a look of disbelief on the lawman's face, then his lips tightened convulsively.

'You sayin' that you shot down Red Kelsey and Clem Arnott in fair fight?'

'That's the truth, Sheriff,' broke in the bartender, evidently proud at this chance to speak up for the man who had outdrawn these two dangerous killers, 'I saw it all. They drew first after tryin' to rile him. Both tried to go for him at the same time.'

The Sheriff eyed Clint with a new sort of respect, but his tone was still hard as he said: 'Reckon there's likely to be hell to pay when the rest of the boys get back to Jess Durman with this news. Red was his foreman. You've sure stirred up a real hornet's nest here, Mister.' His gaze became shrewd. 'You ain't proposin' to stick around town here, I hope?'

'Could be,' Clint nodded. 'Depends on whether I get my business done here or not.'

The Sheriff said sharply, 'I'm not sure that I can allow that, Mister.'

Clint felt a faint amazement at the other's statement. 'You goin' to try to stop me, Sheriff?' His tone was deceptively mild. 'I don't know of any law that says I can't stay here.'

'Well I do,' declared the other in an angry tone. 'I'm the law here. All I have to do is keep things quiet and peaceable in town. If Durman and his boys come into town looking for Red and Clem's killer, he'll not stop until he finds you and he might bust up the whole town lookin'.'

'I reckon that's your problem, not mine, Sheriff,' said Clint casually.

'You're darned right it is,' snapped the other. 'And if the only way I can prevent that from happenin' is to make sure you're out of town, then by golly I mean to do it.'

'You ain't got that authority, Sheriff,' Clint said flatly. 'Seems to me that Durman is the law around here and not you.'

The other's face turned a dull crimson at the implication behind that remark. He gritted his teeth and for an instant, his hand hovered close to the butt of his gun, eyes bright. Then he thought better of the idea that was in his mind, let his hand fall to his side and said thinly: 'You'd better steer clear of any more trouble, mister, so long as you're in town. And if Durman or his men do come ridin' in lookin' for you, I shan't stop 'em.'

'I reckon that's a fair warning, Sheriff,' grunted Clint. He poured one last drink, gulped it down and slid a couple of coins on to the counter, before walking out. At the door, he paused, said to the bartender, 'Any idea where I can get a bed and a meal?'

'Sure thing, mister.' The other nodded. 'There's a hotel across the street. It isn't much, but it's the only place in this town.'

'Thanks.' Clint nodded in acknowledgement, then went out into the dusty street, glancing warily up and down it before stepping down off the boardwalk into the yellow dust. There was a little coolness in the air now, and he relished the faint touch of the breeze on his scorched face. Sucking in a lungful of air, he drew it deeply down inside him, filling his lungs with it. The raw and sun-scorched thoroughfare that ran straight as a die through the middle of the town, was empty now as far as the eye could see in either direction. A quick glance showed him where the hotel was. A small, unpretentious building on the other side of the street, tucked between the small gunsmith's and the bank, it had two storeys but little else to commend it. The windows were small, dusty, with the sunlight glinting off them.

His spurs lifted tiny tufts of dust as he walked over to the hotel, pushed open the door and stepped inside. The sleepy-looking clerk, lounging behind the desk in the lobby eyed him curiously for a long moment, then pushed himself stiffly to his feet.

'You got a room?' Clint asked.

'Si, señor.' The other nodded rapidly. 'How long weel you be staying here?'

'Difficult to say at the moment. Maybe three, four days.'

'That weel be all right,' the other reached behind him, plucked a key from the wooden rack on the wall, and handed it to him. There was no register here to sign. Evidently they had so few people staying here that one was not considered to be necessary. Clint took the key, made his way up the creaking stairs in the direction of the clerk's pointing finger. At the top, he paused to look about him. There was a long corridor evidently stretching away to the rear of the building, with two smaller passages leading at right angles from it. The doors were numbered and he found his room without much difficulty, opening the door, and then locking it behind him.

There was a tall jug in a basin by the window and he poured some of the water into the basin and, stripping off his dusty jacket and shirt, he washed his face and neck, feeling the mask of dust crack on his cheeks, the water stinging his sun-scorched flesh. Then he pulled a fresh shirt from his saddle-roll, put it on and felt a lot better, cleaner.

He shifted position, going over to the window, but not too close, because he wished to look down into the street below without being seen by anyone who might be down there. The territory around this isolated cow-town was a hundred miles of nothing, he thought inwardly, as he lifted his gaze and looked beyond the cluster of houses and wooden shacks out to the stretching, forbidding desert that lay beyond. Here, the territory was even worse than Nevada which was virtually all desert, with no softness, no warm, green valleys and gently rolling hills. But men were coming here, seeking the silver that was buried in the hills, seeking it legally, or killing for it. He built a cigarette, stuck it between his lips and left it there, unlit for a long moment, turning his thoughts over in his mind, now that there was time to think about things. He opened the window with a thrust of his hand. For a moment, the dried out wood, warped by long exposure to the sun, resisted his efforts. Then it gave and he felt the coolness flow into the room, relieving the oppressive heat which had built up there during the day. There was a different smell in the air now, one he recognized instantly. The pleasant smell of rain before any rain actually came. He looked off to the distant horizon, saw the darkening shadow that lay across it, reckoned that the rain would come sometime during the night.

Seating himself in the chair by the open window, he took the tattered map from his pocket and studied it carefully. He was on the point of slipping it back when there came a loud knock on the door. For a moment, he stood irresolute, then went across the room and opened the door. The man who stood outside was fat with an enormous face that broke into a flabby smile as he saw Clint. For the briefest moment, his eyes rested on the scrap of paper in Clint's hand, then he pushed by him and said heartily. 'Forgive me for intruding like this, but I am Bob Peters. I own the hotel and brought this drink for you. On the house, of course.'

'Why, thank you,' Clint went over to the small table, stood as the other poured the drink, noticed that there were two glasses and said. 'Won't you join me, Mister Peters?'

'Thank you.' The other filled his own glass, sank down into the chair, wiping his perspiring face with a large red handkerchief. 'A man of my size gets hot very easily in weather like this,' he explained, then glanced through the window. 'But there will be a change soon. A storm is brewing out yonder.'

'So I noticed,' Clink drank the cool beer, felt it slake his thirst. He tucked the map unobtrusively into his pocket. 'Tell me, do you get many visitors to this town?'

'Very few,' admitted the other. 'Here you will find only the outlaws, the rustlers and perhaps a few of the miners from the hills along the trail. But they do not stay for very long. If they have silver with them, they spend it in the saloon, or lose it at cards. Then they go out again to dig for some more.'

'There must be some rich strikes in these hills if they afford to do that. I'm surprised more folk haven't done that.'

'What is the use? The outlaws take the silver when they wish, the card-sharps get it too. Why should they waste their time digging it out of the ground when they can get it far more easily.'

'I get your point,' Clint nodded. He was beginning to feel just a little uneasy at the other's presence there. He had noticed the bright stare that had entered the man's eyes the minute he had seen that scrap of paper and it was possible that he had recognized it for what it was. He would have to guard it carefully, if he wanted to keep a hold on it.

It was impossible to get rid of the other quickly without appearing to be inhospitable.

'Another drink?' said Peters. 'There's plenty more where this came from and like I said, we see so few visitors here we try to make 'em as welcome as possible when they do come.'

'I've no objection,' Clint said easily. The other poured more into the glasses.

For a moment, there was silence, then with a shrewd look, the other said: 'I hear that you shot down two of Jess Durman's top hands. He isn't goin' to like that.'

Clint gave a wry grin. 'News sure travels fast in this town,' he remarked.

'The bartender at the cantina is a friend of mine. He likes to brag about everythin' that goes on in there and when two of the slickest gunmen are beaten to the draw, that's somethin' to talk about.' The other smiled in a friendly way, showing his white, even teeth and the deep ripples of flesh on his massive chin.

'I noticed that,' Clint said. The uneasiness increased in his mind although he wasn't quite sure why. This man seemed harmless enough on the surface, yet there was something about him which at the moment defied analysis. It was as if he were determined to probe a little more deeply into Clint's affair, though doing it so unobtrusively that he imagined the other had not noticed his obvious interest.

'I saw the rest of the boys ride out of town as if all the devils in hell were on their trail,' grunted the other. 'Reckon it's about time somebody came in who wasn't scared of 'em and showed them where to get off. Durman is gettin' a heap too big for his boots lately. He's tryin' to horn in on the town, sendin' his boys in to make trouble whenever they can.'

'And what is the Sheriff doin' about it?'

'Who — Burnham?' The other gave a sharp braying laugh. 'He's hand in glove with Durman. He jumps whenever Jess gives an order. Never interferes whenever the Durman riders start anythin'. Always in some other part of town. Funny he didn't try to arrest you on a charge of murder after Red and Clem were shot.'

'Figure he might have tried that if the bartender hadn't stood up for me and testified to what really happened. Even then he was all for runnin' me out of town before trouble breaks.'

'He may try to do that yet,' warned the other. 'If the Durman riders come in lookin' for you and figure you're still in town, they'll blow this place apart at the hinges until they've run you to earth.'

'I've had men on my trail before now,' Clint said easily. 'If they want to start trouble, I won't stop 'em.'

'Better think about this,' muttered the other seriously. His shrewd, close-eyed gaze rested long on Clint. He seemed to be turning other things over in his mind while he spoke. 'Ain't no sense in bucking trouble just for the sake of tryin' to prove you're a better man than they are. They'll mean to get you, and it's more'n likely they'll shoot you in the back.'

'Nice, friendly characters,' Clint grinned.

'They're about as friendly as a bunch of rattlers,' warned the other. He emptied his glass, stared at the half-empty bottle for a long moment, then got to his feet, moving over to the window, his back to Clint. There was the distant rumble of thunder along the horizon and the air, flowing in through the window, seemed cooler than it had been even a few minutes earlier.

'I figure you could be doin' with some rest,' he said, after a pause. Turning, he moved to the door. 'Keep the bottle,' he said quietly, jerking a thumb in the direction of the table.

He went out and a moment later, Clint heard the creak of his heavy body on the narrow stairs, moving down. For a moment, Clint waited, then closed the door and turned the key in the lock. A fork-tongued flash of lightning lanced across the swiftly darkening heavens to the east where the clouds were moving quickly across the sky. Making up another cigarette, he shielded his face and lit it, drawing the smoke quickly into his lungs. The other had not mentioned anything about supper here, but he figured it would be ready in less than half an hour's time. In the meantime, he sat by the window, staring out into the growing darkness. Thirty days on the trail wearied a man to the marrow and he was content to relax and smoke. The first raindrops came hissing down as the freshening breeze drove the rain clouds over the town. The sun had vanished in a swirling mass of black cloud and the thunder rumbled and rolled like a beserk animal striding the plateau of the heavens.

Crushing out the butt of the cigarette, he got to his feet, stretched himself and then buckled on the heavy gunbelt, going out into the passage and down the stairs into the lobby. There was no one seated behind the desk when he entered, but after a few moments, he located the dining room to one side and went in, glancing about him. There were half a dozen circular tables dotted around the room, but nobody around. Seating himself at one of the tables against the wall so that he sat facing the door, he leaned back and forced himself to relax. A few moments later, the door opened and the fat man came waddling in, spotted him and came over with a wide grin.

'Just gettin' supper fixed up,' he explained. 'Won't be more'n five minutes. Guess you must be hungry ridin' so long on that trail to the north.'

Clint nodded. Again he felt that the other was trying his best to draw him out and get him to talk more than he intended. 'I could do with a bite to eat,' was all he said.

The other waited for a few moments, evidently hoping that he would say something further. There was a magpie curiosity in his face, head held cocked a little to one side. Then a slight frown crossed his bland features and he turned with an unnatural sharpness and left the dining room. Five minutes passed before he returned with the meal which he placed in front of Clint. The other forced himself to be completely at ease.

After the man had gone, he fell to, eating ravenously, the only person in the dining room. In spite of his earlier misgivings, he was forced to admit that the meal had been excellently prepared.

Not until the last morsel had been eaten, did he sit back, staring down at the coffee in the cup. He drank it slowly, feeling the warmth flow back into his limbs. This was something he had dreamed of all those long weary days and nights on the trail, those cold camps among the trees or in the flat desert, with the sand blowing into his cold food. He had been tired, but now there was a new life in his body. He built himself a cigarette and lit it, was on the point of rising when another figure came into the dining room, threw him a quick questioning glance then walked heavily across, stood in front of him, his gaze resting on the empty chair at the other side of the table.

'Mind if I sit and have a talk?' asked the sheriff quietly.

'Not at all,' Clint said. 'I was just on my way outside for a spell, but judging from that storm which was comin' in from the east, I reckon it's warmer and drier in here.'

The lawman stared down at his wet

jacket, then gave a brief nod. There was still nothing of friendliness about him. He seemed taut and indrawn, with a frown of worried annoyance on his bluff features. 'You still figurin' on staying here, in spite of what happened in the cantina?'

'That was no cause of mine,' Clint pointed out. 'They started that fracas for some reason known only to themselves. I reckon they must've had some reason. I've never seen any of those men before in my life.'

'Could be they figured you for somebody else,' said the other flatly.

'Could be. You got any idea who it might have been?'

The sheriff shook his head ponderously. 'Nope,' he said without emotion. 'If I did, I reckon I might feel a mite easier in my mind than I do right this minute. I'm waiting for all hell to break loose here. This is one hell of a town at the best of times but at the moment it's shelterin' a host of the wild ones and if trouble does start, it won't be easy to stop it. Like a powder keg with a train of gunpowder leadin' up to it. You've lit the fuse whether you know it or not.'

Clint regarded him contemplatively for a while through the haze of blue tobacco smoke. Then he asked: 'Just who is this Jess Durman, anyway? I know he's the biggest rancher in the territory. The bartender told me that but it means very little. I mean what kind of a man is he?'

The sheriff stroked his chin, the bristles rasping under his fingers. His eyes narrowed a little, the thick, bushy brows drawn into a bar-straight line over them. 'He's a mean critter when he's riled,' he said slowly, obviously choosing his words carefully, still not quite sure of the man who faced him across the table. 'He's a big man, owns the biggest spread around these parts and most of the land in the territory. And he didn't get where he is by relyin' on other men. He can use his own gun as fast as any man I've ever seen. You might figure that Red was greased lightning with a gun, but he was slow compared with Jess Durman. I've seen him draw and I don't think there's a man alive to match him.'

'Then I reckon he's a very scared man,' said Clint softly. He saw the look of puzzlement in the other's eyes and went on. 'When a man gets as fast as you say, he's always scared that someday he'll come up against a man who's just that shade faster, that little bit truer and luckier. Then he knows he's goin' to lose out when he faces him. That's why so many men die in the road dust of a hundred towns like this one, die with that look of frozen astonishment on their faces, because you never have the chance to find out how good, how fast, a man is until you've stepped out to face him. Then, it's a little too late to rectify any mistakes you might have made about him.'

'Well ... mabbe so,' growled the other. 'Very likely you're right, but I wouldn't like to be the man to step out and face Jess Durman.'

He sat back in his chair, regarded Clint speculatively from under the lowered brows. He still seemed puzzled. Then he shook his head slowly. 'I'd still like to know what it is that's keepin' you here, mister, when you know that Jess will be ridin' in soon, lookin' for your hide.'

Clint smiled a thin, wintry smile. 'Like I told you before, Sheriff. This is my own personal business. Let's say that I have somethin' to settle because of a man who died on the trail here, shot down from ambush by a crew of killers.'

'A friend of yours?' said the other, glancing up in sudden interest.

'Nope. Never even knew his name. But I still figure I owe him somethin'. I like to see a man get an even break.'

The sheriff gave a quick nod, scraped back his chair and got heavily to his feet. 'Move easy while you're in town,' he warned. 'All strangers comin' in here are watched by everybody and you've started big trouble. Even with me, every time I walk down that street out yonder I wonder when somethin' is goin' to bust wide open.'

'I'll be careful,' Clint told him. He waited until the other had left, then went up to his room. Outside, the storm had almost blown itself out. There were several bright stars showing clearly low down in the east, broken splinters of brilliance against the heaven's dark back-cloth. The air felt cool and moist and he decided to take a walk to the cantina before turning in. Acting on impulse, he took out the map from his pocket and placed it carefully beneath the springs of the bed where it would not be easily found.

Going out, he gave the street a careful study. There was a hoarse shout from somewhere along it, out of sight in the darkness and he ignored it after a moment. He passed two dark stores, moved cautiously across the mouth of an alley that yawned like an empty mouth at him, black and potentially dangerous. In spite of the tight grip he had on himself, he felt jumpy and a little nervous, with that tiny spot between his shoulder blades itching a warning to him. If he was being watched he could see no one in the blackness, but here along this main street there was a score of places where a man might hide and lie in wait for someone who was a little too unwary.

Across the roadway, a shaft of yellow lamplight shone through one of the windows, cutting a swathe of brilliance in the darkness which infested the street. Dark-squared silhouettes of men moving by on the other boardwalk passed across it, the light touching their shadowed faces for an instant. Almost invariably, they turned in at the saloon, the batwing doors swinging loosely shut behind them. At the end of the long storehouse beside him, he stood leaning his back on the building to make himself a cigarette. He felt no urge to smoke, but the cigarette could be used to many other purposes and it gave him a reason for standing idly there while he watched everything in progress. He threw a coldly calculating glance about him for several moments. There was a faint sound of music from inside the saloon, drifting out into the dark, star-strewn night. It swirled around him like an invisible cloud, evoking memories he had long thought to be forgotten.

Stepping down into the dust of the street a moment later, he half smiled to himself in the darkness. The fragment of music stayed with him, and there was the fainter sound of a woman's voice, sweet and low, rising occasionally above the tinkling of the piano and the high-pitched sound of the fiddle.

Lighting the cigarette, he dropped the spent match into the dust and ground it in with his heel. This frontier cow-town was settling down to the night as did all other such towns wherever he had met up with them. The pattern was always the same. Violence could break out at any moment, but in the meantime everybody seemed to be in the best of spirits and if there was any concern about the two gunmen who had been shot down that afternoon in the cantina by the unknown stranger who had just ridden into town, there was little indication of it. For all these people knew Jess Durman might be riding into town that very minute, determined to find and destroy the man who had killed his two best men.

He debated whether to step into the saloon, then decided against it, moved on slowly along the boardwalk, in the shadowed darkness of the buildings, aware of the curious glances he got from the men who moved past him. By now they would know him at least by reputation.

Stepping down off the boardwalk where a narrow alley moved back into the utter blackness which lay over the town away from the main street, he heard a sudden movement in the shadows and someone called softly to him out of the darkness. He stiffened abruptly, strained his gaze, pushing it into the blackness to try to make out the shape of the man who stood there, but he could see nothing beyond the dim, vague shadow, crouched against the wall.

'Whoever you are, step out here where I can see you,' he grated thinly, one hand hovering close to the butt of his gun.

'Don't shoot, mister. I only want to warn you. But if I'm seen, I'll be a dead man for talkin' to you.'

'You'll be a dead man if you don't step out away from that wall and keep your hands well in sight,' Clint said tightly.

The other moved slowly away from the wall. Clint had a vague impression of a bent body and a broad-brimmed hat pulled down well over the other's eyes. The man deliberately kept his hands well away from his sides, stepping out into the middle of the alley. There did not seem to be anything dangerous about him, Clint decided as he took a couple of paces forward, trying to make out the other's features. Probably one of the oldsters in the town who saw everything that went on, siding with nobody so as to stay alive.

'Nothin' to get edgy about,' said the other in a faintly-heard whisper. 'Sorry if I got you jumpy, but this is one hell of a town as you've probably found out. Eyes watchin' everywhere.'

Clint nodded. He stood in front of the other, still wary, alert for danger. 'All right,' he went on tautly. 'What is it you've got to say to me?'

The other murmured something under his breath that Clint did not catch. As he leaned forward to hear better, there was a slight sound at his back and something crashed on the side of his skull, bringing blackness with it.

3

Night Intruder

Deperately, Clint tried to force himself
back to consciousness. He was aware of
a sea of pain washing over him and of
the pounding waves of agony that beat
inside his head. Dull voices drifted to
him out of the darkness around him
and he was vaguely aware of hands
fumbling with his jacket, searching
through his pockets. He tried to fight
against them, tried to force himself up
on to his hands and knees in the
darkness, but there seemed to be no
strength left in his body, his legs were
like water under him and his arms so
heavy that he lacked the power to move
them a single inch.

'Nothin' here,' said a harsh voice
close to his ear. The words seemed to
reach him from a tremendous distance,

receding and then coming closer with a sudden abruptness.

'But it's got to be here,' grunted another voice which, like the first, he did not recognize. 'He's the only one who could have had it. That old fool must have hidden it somewhere along the trail and this *hombre* is the only one who's ridden that trail since then.'

'I tell you there's nothin' here,' snarled the voice again, more angrily now. 'His pockets are empty except for a few coins and tobacco.'

'Then he must've dropped it off someplace, intendin' to go back for it later.'

Clint tried to push up, but his arms would no longer support his body. He felt the blackness coming in again to engulf him, shook his head then gave it up as a splitting spasm of agony lanced through his skull. A voice muttered something he could not make out and there came another shattering impact on the side of his head and this time, he went out like a light and knew nothing for a long time. When he finally came to, it was still dark. Slowly, he opened his eyes, squinted up at the bright sparks of light in front of his face and realized, with a sudden rush of returning clarity, that there were stars, flinging their radiance down at him from the clear heavens. The wind was a drifting coolness on his face. He lay for a long moment, doubting his strength, then pushed himself slowly upright with a tremendous effort. His head throbbed painfully and putting up a hand he touched it gingerly, felt the warm stickiness of blood on the side of his features. He drew in a shuddering breath, forced his eyes to remain open, his brain clearing slowly.

Gradually, memory came back. He recalled that old man standing there in the middle of the alley and cursed himself for having fallen for such an old trick as that, thinking that the old man was the source of the danger, concentrating all of his attention on him while his other assailant had crept up unnoticed behind him and struck him down. They had obviously known he was carrying something valuable and had gone through his pockets carefully. He was thankful he had taken the obvious precaution of hiding that map and the nugget up in his room. Then the thought came to him that perhaps those two men who had tried to rob him might have gone up to his room and were already searching it, looking for that scrap of paper. If he had had any doubts as to its genuineness before, he certainly had none now.

Carefully, slowly, he began to move his arms and legs, flexing his fingers experimentally. The feeling was coming back into them gradually and after a little while he was able to get to his feet and stand without falling. His head continued to throb dully and he stood swaying as the blood rushed, pounding, to his temples. He clung to the wall for support, moving one step at a time towards the main street. The attack had been a warning to him, possibly the first of many, that there were other men who were interested in him, apart from Jess Durman, who only wanted him dead.

How long he had been unconscious in that alley, he did not know. There was still music and singing coming from the direction of the saloon, and a few men on the board-walks who eyed him and then passed by. Somehow, he found his way to the hotel, stumbled through the door into the dim lobby. The clerk sat sleepy-eyed behind the desk, shot him a sharp-bright glance as he made his way slowly up the creaking stairs to his room. Some instinct made him pause outside the door and press his ear close to it, listening for any sound from inside. After a few moments he felt reasonably confident the room was empty. If those men who had jumped him in the alley had come here to search, they had gone.

Turning the key in the lock, he pushed the door open, went inside. In the darkness, he felt his way over to the table, struck a match and lit the paraffin lamp. In the warm yellow glow, he looked about him, half expecting to see the room ransacked, but everything seemed to be as he had left it. Before doing anything else, he went over to the window, pulled the shutters into place. It was then he found that the lock on the windows did not work and that the catch had been broken. There was also a long balcony outside which ran around the building. The perfect set-up for anyone to enter during the night, he reflected.

He wondered if the clerk had deliberately arranged for him to have this room. It was something worth considering, he thought, as he pulled the wooden shutters as far over as he could, then went back to the bed and felt for the paper and silver nugget. Both were there and he pulled them out, regarding them in the pale yellow glow with more than curiosity now. One man had already died for these and a similar attempt had been made on his life.

Locking the door, he washed some of the blood from his face, felt a little better, his mind a little clearer than before. He wondered again about Peters, the man who owned this hotel. The other had undoubtedly seen that paper, had probably guessed what it was. On impulse, he pulled one of his Colts from its holster when he turned in and slipped it under his pillow, lying so that he faced the window, confident that it would be from this direction that any danger would come through the night.

* * *

Something, some tiny sound, reached down into the part of Clint's mind which never slept, waking him, his mind alert as he lay there on the low bed, straining with his ears and narrowed eyes in the darkness of the room, seeking the cause of his wakening. For a moment, there was nothing. Then he heard the faint sound once more, almost immediately outside the shuttered window. He sat bolt upright on the bed, heard the stealthy movement on the balcony, then slid silently from the bed and padded over to the corner of the room, the Colt hard and cold in his hand, his finger resting bar-straight on the trigger. Gradually, his eyes grew accustomed to the pitch blackness. He could just make out the faint outlines of the table in the middle of the room and the faint chinks of light around the edges of the shutters across the windows. It would be moonlight outside now, he thought tightly, enabling whoever was out there to see clearly.

There was the sound of heavy breathing outside on the balcony and he knew that the intruder was standing directly behind the shutters, waiting patiently to make sure there was no sound from inside the room. Then, with a faint creak, the shutters were pushed open from the outside as a knife blade was carefully inserted between them, lifting the lock where it had been deliberately broken so that they could not be secured.

How many other travellers, staying in this hotel, had been robbed in a similar fashion, Clint wondered, unable to prove a thing in the morning, possibly not daring to make too strong an accusation in this town for fear of their own lives. The shutters opened and in the faint stream of moonlight that filtered through into the room, he made out the fat shape which eased its way through the gap in the windows, stepping down into the room with a silence and lightness that belied the bulk.

Clint waited until the other had begun to edge forward, moving in the direction of the bed. He saw the man peer forward, straining his head as he tried to make out anyone lying on the bed. Then he must have realized that for the first time he had walked right into a trap for his hand moved down towards his belt and he began to turn.

'Hold it!' Clint snapped. He moved out into the room and rammed the barrel of the Colt into the small of the other's back, felt the metal sink into the flabby flesh there. The man uttered a sharp, high-pitched bleat of agony as the foresight ground into him.

'That's better.' Reaching round, Clint removed the gun from the other's belt. 'I figured you might come to pay me a visit sometime durin' the night,' he said quietly. 'When I found it wasn't possible to lock the windows and noticed the balcony running all the way around the building, it was obvious why this had been done. I suppose you make a good haul from many of your visitors this way.'

'Now don't get me wrong,' began the other harshly. Even in the dim moonlight, Clint could see the streams of sweat runnelling down the man's flabby features, shining in the light. 'I'll admit this doesn't look too good. So I made a mistake, but there was nothin' in it, I assure you.'

'Just what did you figure I might have here that was worth stealin'?'

'Why — nothin'.' It was clear from the other's tone, that he was lying. Clint wondered if Peters knew of the map and the silver nugget and if he did, how he had come to hear about them.

'Don't lie to me, Peters,' he snapped, digging in harder with the gun. 'You had some reason for breakin' in here.'

'I figured you might be carrying some gold,' said the other through thinned lips. 'So I was wrong. What you goin' to do. Turn me over to the sheriff?'

'I'd do that if I thought it would do any good. But he's no more the law in this town than I am. But I'm warnin' you, Peters. Try a trick like this once more, and the next time there'll be a bullet waitin' for you.'

He felt the other stiffen. Peters licked his lips, then backed towards the door as Clint prodded him across the room. Turning the key in the lock, Clint opened the door, thrust the other out of the room and into the corridor. 'Better heed my warnin', Peters,' he said harshly. 'I don't give second warnings.'

Closing the door, he locked it once more. Going back into the room, he stretched himself out on the low bed once more, listening to the faint sounds inside the building, wondering whether he had done the right thing by letting the other off so lightly. He shifted unomfortably on the bed, worried by his thoughts and realized that he had been holding himself tense by listening, every nerve and muscle strained so that it produced a deep-seated ache in the whole of his body. Movement made him painfully aware of the bruises and aches in his limbs. He did not think that Peters would try anything like that again but he slept with the pistol under his pillow, ready to snatch it out and use it if he was forced to do so.

But there was no further incident during the night and he was wakened by the brilliant sunlight streaming in through the gap in the shutters where he had forgotten to close them again.

Sitting up in bed, he felt that sudden clamour in his head again, as if half a dozen blacksmiths were hammering away at his brain, sending out showers of white-hot sparks that danced at the back of his eyelids. With an effort, squeezing up his eyes, he managed to force them away. Slowly his whole being steadied, the room stopped its tilting and swaying around him. He swung his legs to the floor and managed to stand upright without holding on to anything.

He made his way down to the dining room. There was no sign of Peters and it was a small Mexican woman who brought him in his breakfast, set it down on the table in front of him without a word and then left, moving out of the room as silently as she had entered. He ate slowly, chewing every mouthful carefully, trying to turn things over in his mind so that they made some kind of sense, no matter how far-fetched it might be. He recalled how he had been attacked the previous night in that alley. But when his assailants had discovered nothing on him, they had made no attempt to go up to his room and search there although that would have seemed the logical thing for them to do. Had it been because they knew they could leave that to Peters — that he would be able to enter his room without arousing too much suspicion, that all three men were in this together.

He glanced up as a shadow fell over the table. Sheriff Burnham stood looking down at him, an oily grin on his face. He said tersely: 'Looks to me as though you've been in some kinda trouble, mister?'

'Nothin' I can't handle,' Clint said easily. He motioned to the other chair. 'Though I guess you haven't stepped over just to inquire about my health.'

'You guess right,' Burnham nodded. 'You're a hard man to kill. I heard about that attack on you in the alley last night. They could've finished you for good in there, you know.'

'I know. I've been wonderin' for some time now why they didn't,' Clint said seriously, brows knit in a faintly puzzled frown.

'Could be because they figure they'll need you alive to tell them what they want to know,' said the other through pursed lips.

'And what is that supposed to mean?' Clint sipped the hot coffee slowly, eyeing the sheriff over the rim of the cup.

Burnham grimaced slightly. 'The way I figure it, you've got somethin' these men want pretty bad. I've no idea what it is, but they'll go to any lengths to get their hands on it. Now it's clear they didn't find it on you when they jumped you in the alley, so I reckon whatever it is you still have it hidden away someplace.' He eyed Clint keenly, as though watching for any little gust of expression that might flash across his face as he spoke.

'You seem to have plenty of ideas in your head, Sheriff,' Clint forced a quick grin. 'Though they're pretty wild ones right now.'

'Are they?' For a moment, Burnham eyed him closely, then sat back in his chair, stretching his legs out straight in front of him. There was a tight, hard look on his unshaven face. 'I've seen men ride in here who had plenty to hide. Men who figured that this kind of cow-town was just the place for folk keepin' one jump ahead of the law where nobody would ask questions and they'd be able to keep out of the way of anybody comin' in on their trail.'

'Now you ain't tryin' to tell me there's some kinda law and order around here, Sheriff,' Clint looked at the other in mild surprise. 'After what happened yesterday in the cantina, I don't believe you.'

Burnham tightened his lips then sucked in a deep gust of air, blowing out his cheeks. 'I told you I don't want any trouble around here,' he said angrily. 'Now I mean that. Don't you go startin' anythin' else or I'll have to lock you up or shoot you down. I appreciate your feelings after what happened, but until we know more about the reasons behind this, take things easier, huh?'

Clint rose stiffly, stood looking down at the other. Keeping a tight rein on his anger, he said through clenched teeth and thinned lips. 'I warned those men with Red and Clem that I'd go gunnin' for 'em if they ever tried to rile me again and by golly I meant it.' He went out, leaving the sheriff staring after him with his face flushed red under the two-day stubble.

Outside in the street, he hesitated, staring up and down the roadway, glaring in the harsh sunlight. The mud which had formed under the heavy rains of the previous evening was already baked hard by the heat, and there were long cracks in it, splintering under his boots as he walked down the very centre of the street, eyes flicking from one side to the other. He went inside the small cantina. Somehow he had the feeling that he could perhaps trust the bartender there a little way, although the mere fact that the other had talked about the shooting to Peters, told against him. Still, the swarthy Mexican was one man who might be able to help him now, give him some information.

The other eyed him warily as he walked inside. The cantina was empty except for a trio of Mexicans in one corner, seated around a table, two of them with their heads bowed on their arms as though asleep, the other leaning back in his chair, staring straight in front of him as though looking at something too distant for anyone else to see.

'I thought you would have ridden out last night, *señor*,' said the other slowly, setting the bottle in front of him. 'You are beeg fool to stay here, waiting for trouble.'

Clint frowned. 'You know this territory well?' he asked abruptly.

If the other was surprised at the sudden switch of question, he gave no outward sign of it, merely nodded dully. 'I live here all my life. I know all of the trails, although now there ees no reason for me to ride them. I stay here and listen to the talk of the others.'

'Good,' Clint nodded his head slowly. He decided to take a chance. 'You ever hear of a silver mine up in the hills somewhere called the El Dorado Mine?'

He saw the tight glitter that flashed at the back of the other's eyes, knew that the name had struck a responsive chord in the other's mind. 'What have you heard of the El Dorado Mine, *señor*?' His voice was little more than a hushed whisper now that only travelled to Clint, no further. He leaned his elbows on the bar and rested his weight on them.

'You know it then?' asked Clint indirectly.

The man nodded. His lips worked for a moment before he could trust himself to speak. 'It was one of the richest silver mines in the whole territory. But the man who found it, a crazy gringo called Webber, died without tellin' anyone where it was located. They say that he drew a map of its whereabouts and gave it to the man who found him dying of thirst in the desert, a man called Everett.'

Clint poured himself a drink and threw it down quickly. That man he had found with the bullet in him among the rocks in the wastelands — had he been Everett? It seemed more than probable.

'You think this map exists?'

'It could be,' agreed the other. 'But if it does, and this man Everett has it, his life is worth very little. Too many men have gone out looking for that mine and the silver in it, and too many men have died.'

That too, was logical, Clint thought. He drank his second drink more slowly, pondering on it. The two men who had jumped him knew he had that map somewhere. He stood against the bar and tried to recall exactly what the words were that he had heard dimly when they had searched through his pockets for the map. Something about him having the map since he was the only man to have ridden that trail. So it was possible those men had either been in the bunch that had shot down Everett along the trail, or they had somehow discovered about it and had him figured as the new owner of the map to the El Dorado Mine.

He felt a tight grimness in him as he finished his drink. Maybe if he was to start pushing things a little, he might force these men out into the open. This trail that led on south through Durman's ranch was the silver trail he had heard about further north. A trail that was watched by more outlaws and gunslingers than one could count. Whether or not Durman was in on this outlawry was something he did not know at the moment, although that bunch of men who had been with Red and Clem when they had called him out to fight had looked typical killers. With a ranch that straddled the trail,

Durman was sure in a good position to keep an eye on things and if the miners had to come through his land on their way into town, he had a better chance than anyone else of jumping them and relieving them of any silver they might be carrying. The more he figured it out, the more it seemed to make some kind of sense.

Going out of the cantina, he stepped down into the street. He was on the point of going back up into the hotel when he heard the sound of riders coming into town at a fast pace. Glancing behind him, he saw the dust lifted by their horses and a moment later, they came into view, riding swiftly along the main street. A gun blasted and a moment later, there was a regular chorus of gunshots breaking out as they came on at a swift trot until they reined in front of the saloon. Clint watched them through narrowed eyes, still not quite sure who they were. Then a voice close beside him said sharply,

'You'd better get off the street,

mister. That's Jess Durman and his crew.'

Clint swung, saw a short, black-whiskered man standing by one of the wooden uprights outside the hotel. The man was dressed in a frock coat, might have been a gambler or a lawyer from the look of him.

'Thanks for the warnin'.' Clint said. He stepped up on to the boardwalk beside the other.

'I figure you may be the man they're lookin' for.' The other gave a brief smile that showed his teeth. 'You are this man, Lanner who shot Red Kelsey and Clem Arnott?'

'I'm Clint Lanner,' he acknowledged. 'Looks as though Durman won't trust himself to do this business. He had to bring his crew along with him to back any play he may make.'

'He always keeps in the background if there's likely to be big trouble,' said the other. 'He's mighty fast with a gun himself, but you can be sure that when he calls anybody out, he's got a pat hand and he's leaving nothing to chance.'

'And what might your interest be in this?' asked Clint narrowly, struck by a sudden suspicion that ticked at his mind.

'Me, sir?' There was a note of astonishment in the man's voice. 'I merely like to see a man given an even chance. Those men will shoot you in the back if they get the opportunity. Don't ever underestimate Durman and his men. All of them are professional killers, hired for one purpose. To do his dirty work for him and see that he doesn't have to worry about anything. When you gunned down Red and Clem, you dealt him a blow from which he'll find it hard to recover and so long as you are on the loose, he has you figured as a potential source of danger to his continued livelihood.'

'Well now,' Clint said, with the first faint beginnings of a smile on his lips. 'What would you suggest I should do right now? Turn and run?'

'They'll be lookin' for you as soon as they've slaked their thirst after that ride from the ranch.'

The men had gone into the saloon now, with the single exception of the man who sat the big bay horse outside the building. He was tall and slender, with a hard face, the brim of his hat pulled well down on his forehead to shade the eyes from the sun. He sat quite still, then suddenly wheeled his mount and rode slowly along the street until he passed in front of the sheriff's office. He hesitated a moment, then swung from the saddle and walked inside. Clint remained where he was for a moment, then stepped into the hotel.

★ ★ ★

He ate dinner in the dining room of the hotel. There was the possibility that he might have got something to eat in the cantina, but he doubted if the food there would have been as good and he knew that sooner or later, there might

105

be trouble and this time, he wanted it to come on ground of his own choosing. He was not quite sure what was in Durman's mind at that moment. Certainly the other had made no move since he had arrived in town that morning and as far as Clint was aware the gunslingers he had brought with him were still holed up in the saloon.

He had just finished his dinner and was relaxing in his chair, building himself a smoke when the dining room door opened and a man stood in the doorway looking about him with a flat, curious stare. A large man with sharp blue eyes that took in everything, his gaze travelling around the room before it lighted on Clint. The other was aware of the sudden tightening of the man's mouth, the way the lines around his eyes deepened. Then the other came forward, stood in front of him, legs braced well apart, before reaching up with his left hand and thumbing the hat back on his head.

'You must be either a fool or a very

brave man,' the big man said. He held his keen gaze on Clint's face, cool and appraising as if a little unsure what to make of him.

'Let's suppose that you make up your mind about that, Mister Durman,' Clint said softly.

The other gave a tight grin. 'So you know who I am.'

'That's right. I saw you ride in with that bunch of gunhawks. You must be a man who never takes chances to come ridin' in with those men at your back.' If the other felt any anger at that remark, he did not show it. The words seemed to flow off him like water from a duck's back. His gaze did not alter either and the remark seemed to interest him rather than anger him.

'Mind if I sit down?'

'Help yourself. The dinner here is pretty good. Better than you'll get at the saloon or the cantina.'

'I'm not interested in eating at the moment,' said the other quietly, his tone flat and lacking in emotion. 'You and I have some straight talkin' to do, I reckon. I hear you shot down two of my boys in the cantina.'

'You heard right,' said the other evenly. 'They called me out and I shot 'em down in self-defence.'

'I'm not doubting it.' The other nodded a little, still not taking his gaze from Clint's face. 'But you know that caused me a lot of trouble. I need men I can trust, men who know how to use their guns when the necessity arises. Both Red and Clem were good men and I can ill-afford to lose them.'

'Maybe you should have warned 'em not to go callin' out men they don't know. That can be the death of a lot of men.'

Durman considered this, was briefly silent. A hint of hard irony appeared down around his mouth, tightening his lips a little into a thin line. 'You a little jumpy, maybe with the law on your tail?' he inquired. The shade of interest in his eyes spread down and touched the rest of his face.

'Nope, I'm not. But I don't like being called out by men I don't even know.'

'Let's say that was a mistake. They probably figured you for somebody else. It's a mistake anybody can make.'

'It's likely to be the last mistake anybody makes,' Clint told him. He felt puzzled by the other's attitude. He had expected this man to send in his boys to hunt him down, and instead he was talking with him as if nothing had happened. Just what was on Durman's mind? he wondered tightly. Was there a little more to this than he knew? Certainly it seemed like it at the moment.

'You lookin' for a job at all?' asked the other suddenly, his tone a trifle sharp.

'Not particularly,' Clint eyed him with a stiff jolt of a glance. 'Why? You lookin' for somebody to take Red's place?'

'Could be. I need a man who knows how to handle a gun and I pay well. A hundred a month and all found. You'll find that if you work for me you'll be safe from any lawmen who might come ridin' through this territory.'

'I sort of figured that,' Clint said ironically. He checked the sudden inclination to push back his chair, get to his feet, and walk deliberately away from the other, letting him know what he thought about this offer. From beneath his lowered lids, he continued to study Durman. There was that touch of arrogance to the other which showed him to be a man who gave the orders and expected to have them all obeyed to the letter.

Deep inside, he could feel a hardness of his own rising in him. He checked on the sharp rejoinder that rose unbidden to his lips, said steadily. 'I ain't lookin' for a job right now, Mister Durman. I've got some business to take care of in these parts and — '

'You turnin' down my offer?' There was a little snap to the other's voice. 'I suppose you know the alternative?'

'Get to the point,' Clint snapped

harshly. 'I don't feel in the mood for riddles.'

The other's brows drew together into a hard line. He said thinly, his tone loaded with menace. 'Like I said, I've got a place for a man like you in my outfit. I'm willin' to forget the past, forget about Red and Clem. But if you turn down that offer, then my boys will be lookin' for you. They thought a lot about those two men you shot down and I reckon you won't live to see the morning.'

'I don't take kindly to threats as your men found out to their cost' Clint said. This time he did get to his feet, standing with his weight resting on his knuckles on the table. 'I warned those men of yours that the next time I saw 'em, I'd come gunnin' for 'em. Seems to me they've forgotten.'

He turned sharply on his heel, went out of the diner. At the door, he paused and glanced back. Durman had scarcely moved. He sat in the chair at the table, staring directly in front of him. Only the tight-knuckled grip of his fingers on the edge of the table testified to the thoughts that were running through his mind at that particular moment. Clint's words and actions had cut him to the quick. Nothing would stop him from sending his men on an errand of vengeance some time that afternoon or evening. He might leave it until after dark, to add to the fun.

In his room, Clint went over to the window, stood a little to one side so that he might not be spotted from the street and watched the scene below. A few moments passed and then the tall figure of Jess Durman came out of the hotel immediately below him, paused to throw a quick glance in the direction of his room, then continued on his way across to the saloon a little further along the street. A wind had sprung up, whipping the dried dust from the street and sending it in whirling eddies along the street along with tumbling bundles of green-brown sage brush, blown in from the desertlands on the outskirts of town.

After Durman had gone into the saloon, the street remained quiet. It was a little after high noon and the full blaze of the harsh glaring sun lay on the town. A dog dragged itself out of the patch of blistering sunlight into one of the shadows and lay with its tongue hanging between its teeth, belly rising and falling as it drew air into its body, ribs showing clearly under the tight flesh.

He waited by the window for several minutes and when Durman didn't come out with his men at his back, he knew they would do little before dark, and went back to the bed, stretching himself out on it, building a smoke, lighting it, staring up at the ceiling. He did not doubt that Durman would carry out his threat of turning his crew loose in town, with orders to hunt him down, bring him in, dead or alive, preferably the latter.

★ ★ ★

The cow-town lay deathly hushed in the flooding yellow moonlight. Clint moved easily out of the rear door of the hotel, out into the narrow, rubbish-filled alley that lay at the back of the building, then cut east along the passage which was so narrow in places, that he could barely squeeze through. He doubted if there would be any of the local inhabitants abroad just now. This was no ordinary night. Everybody in town knew why Durman and his men were in town. They were out to kill Clint Lanner and those who had no business in the hunt, including Sheriff Burnham, had found something to do indoors, or in the saloon and they would not venture forth until the gunfighting was over.

Clint cut to his right along a board-walk that was rotten from long misuse. He paused tautly as a loose board creaked loudly under his foot. For a second, his heart had jumped hammering into his throat and his guns were out, eyes flicking in every direction, ready to fire at the slightest movement in the vicinity, but the sound seemed to have passed unnoticed. He had little idea at the moment where Durman's boys were. It wasn't likely they had split up into small groups. After Red and Clem had been killed, they would be a little wary about that, would prefer to remain in a large group, standing a better chance of survival that way.

Behind the hotel and a little off to one side, was a small square opening among the buildings but with the layered shadows lying on it, no moonlight managed to penetrate here and he stood stone-still in the stillness, feeling about him with his eyes and ears, tensed, every muscle and fibre in his body stretched almost to breaking point as he searched the shadows. Total silence closed down about him. It was as if the entire town lay poised on the brink of an abyss of silence so utterly deep that it was afraid of sound. Then, somewhere in the near distance, a horse snickered. Instantly, Clint whirled in the direction of the sound, pressing himself against the wall at his back.

For a long moment, there was nothing. Had it been only a horse that had got tired of being tethered? Or was there something more to it than that? In his position, he couldn't afford to take chances. Swiftly, he moved to one side of the open square, keeping his body pressed well in to the wall. He caught the sudden movement at the very edge of his vision, whirled, his finger tightening down on the trigger.

In that same instant, a voice reached him from the darkness. 'Do not shoot, my friend.'

For the barest fraction of a second, the other's life hung in the balance, then Clint released the pressure on the trigger, stepped forward, a sharp curse on his lips. 'Goddamnit to hell, mister, I nearly shot you down. What in tarnation are you doing skulkin' there in the shadows?'

'There are things I reckon you ought to know,' said the other, moving out into the open. His frock-coat slapped against him in the breeze and his face peered up earnestly at Clint. There was a tiny hint of malicious amusement in his tone as he said: 'They are gathering on the other side of town, working their way in this direction. In less than half an hour, they will have flushed you out and then will come the showdown.'

'And why did you risk your life just to come to tell me this?' asked Clint pointedly.

'Like I said, I like a man to get an even chance. I figured that you might need an extra gun with you when they do come.'

'This is no quarrel of yours, mister,' Clint told him sharply. 'Better get back to where you belong. These men are killers and they won't stop just for you.'

'Evidently you doubt my prowess with a gun,' said the other, his voice gone suddenly soft.

'No, but I don't want you around when the firing starts. You'll only get in the way and make things more difficult for me. Thanks for your warnin', but this is my fight, and nothin' to do with you.'

'Are you really so anxious to die, mister?' The other shook his head in the dimness. 'It would be so easy to get out of this in one piece.'

'How? Hit the trail out of town and make a run for it?'

'In a way — yes.' The other's carefully modulated tone was beginning to grate on Clint's nerves a little and he found himself openly disliking the other, not really trusting him. 'There are a couple of horses tethered less than twenty yards along the street towards the edge of town. We would reach them before those gunhawks get within half a mile of here and once we're out on the trail I know a place where we could shack up until Durman gets tired of waitin' for you to show up again and rides out to his own place.'

A sudden shout came from the centre of the town. There was a solitary gunshot and then silence, crowding swiftly on the heels of the strophying echoes which ran over the town.

'Listen,' said the other with a note of urgency in his tone. 'Already they are getting nervous and trigger-happy, seeing you in every shadow. It will not be long before they get here and then what are your chances going to be? They'll cut you down before you know where they are. Is that what you want? A man has pride, I know, but that ain't no reason for him to throw his life away just because he's too goddamned stubborn to know when he doesn't have a chance at all.'

Clint stared hard at the other. There was something at the back of what the little man said that grated a little on his mind, but he couldn't put his finger on it, and it worried him more than he cared to admit, even to himself. There was sense in what the other said and if he really did have those two horses ready and saddled, there was a good chance of getting clean away. But where was the other's interest in this? He could not see this man going to all of this trouble and possibly risking his neck into the bargain, just because he wanted Clint to get an even chance. He had some other iron in the fire and Clint wished that he knew just what it was.

Another shot blasted out of the darkness, nearer this time and after a brief pause, there was more deep-throated shouting and yelling as the Durman riders went on the rampage through the streets, searching for him with vengeance in their minds.

'All right,' he said suddenly, making up his mind. 'Lead the way to these two horses of yours and no tricks, mind. If you're figurin' on turnin' me over to Durman, I'll put a bullet into you before you do it.'

'Quickly then, this way,' hissed the other. It was as if he had not heard the undisguised threat. He turned and led the way through the dark, moon-thrown shadows on this edge of town, moving from one alley to another, a man certain and sure of his way. Clearly the other had been in this town for some time to be able to move around like this.

Less than five minutes later, they came out of a dark, shadow-filled alley into a wider street. There were the shapes of two horses standing patiently in front of a wide tethering rope and the man nodded towards them. 'Just like I said,' he muttered.

A sudden yell sparked off another volley of crashing gunfire. Involuntarily, Clint whirled but the other caught urgently at his arm, swung him round. 'Keep moving. They're still shooting at shadows.'

Clint remembered his horse back in the livery stable. But there was no call at the present time to go back for his mount. He had the large silver nugget and the map tucked away safely in the pocket of his jacket and what he had left behind in that room at the hotel was of little value, would scarcely be missed, even if he was unable to return for it. He wasn't through with this town yet, he told himself fiercely as he climbed up into the saddle.

The other pulled himself up stiffly as though not used to much riding, threw a quick look along the street and then said softly: 'Let's move. They'll be reaching this side of town soon.' He said this so intently as to swing Clint's gaze over to him.

Slowly, they walked their horses along the street, through another dark alley which cut off to their left, and then out into the main street right on the very edge of town. Still no sign from behind them that they had been seen.

'This way,' said the other tersely, speaking in a hoarse whisper. He led the way past the last few buildings, then out on to the mesa; a vast plain that shone eerily in the bright washing of yellow moonlight.

Clint glanced swiftly over his shoulder. Another yell split the silence, but it was distant and clearly unconnected with them. Now that they were a hundred yards or so from the town, he could just make out the buildings in the distance, a tumbled mass of black shadow sprawling on either side of the wide trail. A few lights showed and the roads through the town shone like silver where the moonlight caught the grey-white dust.

A shot sounded to be repeated from another part of town. The echoes chased themselves among the houses. The Durman boys were moving slowly through the town on a wide front, missing nothing, determined not to let him slip through their fingers and backtrack behind them. But they had not considered the possibility that he might run which was why they had not posted anyone along the trails leading out of town to cut him down if he did try to head into the mesa. The thought of those grim-faced riders hunting him down through the quiet, moon-shadowed streets of the town disturbed him anew. He sucked air into his lungs, threw a quick, appraising glance at his companion. The man's face was in shadow as he rode, sitting straight and stiff in the saddle.

As if aware of his gaze, the other half-turned and said thickly: 'I figure we ought to be safe now. They'll maybe keep looking for you until morning and then call off the hunt when they don't find you.' He fell silent for a moment, contemplating the trail that lay ahead of them. Then he asked: 'You didn't have to leave anything valuable behind you at the hotel when we pulled out so sudden, did you?'

Clint narrowed his eyes momentarily. A little imp of suspicion tacked at the edge of his mind at the other's words, innocent as they had sounded. Then he shook his head slowly. 'Only my bedroll and my horse.'

The man grinned, glanced at the mount Clint rode. 'I reckon fair exchange ain't no robbery,' he muttered.

A hundred yards further on they turned off the main trail over the plain, began to climb into the western slopes of a rocky plateau which lifted with a sharp abruptness from the smoothness of the mesa. The horses frequently slowed, knowing their own pace and for the moment, with no real urgency in their flight from the town, they did not push them. The night air was cold now, the sky clear above them, with the stars foaming down the firmament to the far distant horizons.

Almost half a mile from town, Clint suddenly paused, then reached out with a faint hiss of warning, caught urgently at the other's sleeve. He peered narrowly at the shadowed bank of rock to either side, then shoved his mount back against the left hand bank of rock thus to be absorbed by the black shadows of it.

'What is it?' muttered his companion softly, pulling at the small gun in his pocket.

'Somebody up there. I'm sure of it,' Clint pointed. One of the shadows suddenly detached itself from the tumbled mass of rocks and moved out towards the edge of the trail where it twisted around a sharp bend. The shadow climbed slowly to the flat top of a large boulder, hunkered down on its heels. There was a rifle in the man's hands which he laid down on the smooth rock beside him. A moment later, there was the scrape of a match, a brief yellow flare as the other cupped his hands to his face and lit the cigarette which dangled between his lips. The sharp fragrance of tobacco smoke drifted back to them on the wind.

So Durman had decided to take no chances, Clint reflected grimly, and they had been so sure he would not have these trails watched they had almost ridden into that lookout before they had spotted him. He felt a little shiver go through him, and his fingers tightened momentarily on the reins. This man had clearly been left by the rancher to watch for anybody trying to slip out of town during the night.

Leaning forward, he placed his lip close to his companion's ear.

'Stay here,' he ordered brusquely. 'I'll deal with this. I want to scout around and make sure that this *hombre* is alone before I take care of him.'

The other started to say something, then choked it off rapidly as Clint slid from the saddle and padded noiselessly into the rocks. Occasionally, the trail's turnings cut across the rocks, leaving open stretches of ground free from shadow. He avoided these whenever possible, only to re-orientate himself at times, always watching the man on the rock. The other sat a little distance from the trail, eyes alert as he scanned the road back to town. Had it not been for the fact that he had earlier been some distance below the lip of the trail, he must surely have seen them heading in that direction.

From a distance, the other seemed utterly relaxed as he sat there, smoking, as if anticipating no real trouble. Finally, Clint was satisfied that the man was alone. It made sense. Durman was not expecting him to run without turning and fighting. He had put this man here only on the off-chance that he might turn and run when the showdown came, hoping to save his skin by flight. The mere fact that the man was here, guarding this trail up through the hills and not the more open trail across the mesa said as much. A fleeing man would take to the hills rather than head into open country, even though he could make better time; for on the mesa he would make a far better target.

Shifting position was no longer an easy matter. The man on the flat-topped rock kept turning his head, peering in every direction, clearly not content simply to watch the road leading back into the town. Passing downgrade a little, he moved carefully so as to keep the rocky ledge between the other and himself. He wasn't sure what the man who had ridden with him was doing, whether he had remained behind where he had told him, whether he or his mount might make a slight sound that would give them away.

He came up behind the other, less than twenty feet away, so that the man was between him and the moon. The other's back was towards him, but at that moment, the gunman threw the butt of the cigarette down and straightened up, picking up the rifle and turning slowly. He made a perfect target, standing there, silhouetted against the bright moonlight. Clint edged forward but in his forward impetus and narrowing concentration, his foot touched a loose rock, sent it rattling loudly down the slope. The sound seemed unnaturally loud in the clinging stillness among the rocks. He saw at once the man turning swiftly, pivoting on his heels, bringing up the rifle even as he moved. The gunman's hand did not attempt to lift, it twisted at the wrist, minimising movement and bringing the rifle barrel to bear on Clint's chest. From that distance, it was almost impossible for him to miss.

Twin muzzle-blasts exploded almost together. The shattering echoes ran tumultuously among the rocks, bouncing off the rocky walls of the trail, back to the man who sat his mount a few yards away.

The gunman stretched up as if trying to lift the rifle clear to the heavens, then he toppled forward, his head and shoulders striking the edge of the boulder with a sickening thud as he fell. He dropped out of sight, his body rolling down the slope on to the trail.

Clint moved forward slowly, glanced down, saw the man lying in a heap of tumbled shadow among the loose rocks and shale down below him. Slowly, he holstered his gun, climbed down on to the trail, went forward and turned the other over on to his back, bending on one knee to peer into the dead man's face. He recognized him almost at once as one of the men he had seen with Red Kelsey and Clem Arnott when he had shot down the two gunhawks in the cantina. That cleared up the one point.

Durman had been taking no chance on him getting away from the town.

Straightening up, he moved back into the shadows, to where the frock-coated man sat waiting in the saddle. He was almost level with the other, when the man moved his mount from the shadows.

'Is he dead?' asked the quiet voice from the darkness.

'Yeah, he's dead all right,' Clint said in a weary tone. He moved to his horse, then stopped as the other said.

'All right, get your hands up where I can see them.'

There was a small Derringer in the man's hands now.

4

Treachery

Perplexity settled swiftly over Clint's face. For a long moment, he stood absolutely still in the middle of the trail. Then he noticed the look in the other man's eyes, a look he had seen on several occasions before, greed and avarice, a brilliant glint. The Derringer did not waver an inch as he held it on the man in front of him.

'Just what is this?' said Clint hoarsely.

'Unbuckle that gunbelt of yours and let it drop slowly,' ordered the other, as if he had not heard the question. Clint hesitated, saw the sudden hardening of the other's features and knew that he would shoot him down without compunction if he did not obey. Slowly, he unfastened the buckle, let the gunbelt fall with a clatter at his feet.

'Good. Now step away from it, out into that patch of moonlight where I can see you,' grated the other.

Clint took three steps away from the gunbelt, stood with his hands hanging loosely by his sides. For a moment, he debated whether to make a try for the other's gun, then knew that it would be hopeless. Whoever this man was, he knew how to handle a gun and could probably shoot straight and quick if he had to. This had clearly been planned all along the line. He had pretended to throw in his lot with him to get him out here, away, from Durman and his bunch of hired killers, so that he might get his hands on the map. For a moment he stared up at the harsh, grinning face of the man who sat the horse close by; and then he knew why there had been something oddly familiar about the other, something which had nagged at the back of his mind ever since they had met. This, he knew with a sudden certainty, was the man who had enticed him into that alley when he

133

had been knocked on the head from behind. Was he double-crossing his companion? The man's next words tended to confirm this. 'Now dig out that map you're carryin', mister and let me have it. And I'll take that nugget of silver you have along with it.'

'I don't know what you're talkin' about,' Clint snarled. 'If this is a holdup, you'll find nothin' worth takin' on me.'

'Don't make me have to kill you,' went on the other in a glacial tone. 'I'm not a man of violence, but I intend to have that map. If you won't hand it over to me, then I shall kill you and take it. The choice is entirely yours.'

Clint mastered a sudden spasm of anger that boiled through him. Gritting his teeth, cursing himself inwardly for not having seen this treachery, he dug down into his pocket, pulled out the crumpled piece of paper and the silver nugget and held them out.

'Toss them on to the ground in front of you,' ordered the other harshly.

Clint did as he was told, not once taking his eyes off the other as the man swung down from the saddle. The other jerked the Derringer up to cover him as he took an involuntary step forward. 'Don't try anything foolish,' snapped the other. 'I've been trying to get my hands on this map for a long time and your life means nothing to me compared with this.'

There was something in his tone that told Clint how useless it would be to try to stop the other. He was forced to stand futilely back as the man edged forward, stood regarding him for a moment with a wide, searching stare, then said. 'Turn around.'

Clint hesitated and the other repeated his order more forcefully, stepping close to him. Slowly, Clint turned until his back was towards the other. He heard a faint chuckle from the man at his back and then the butt of the small Derringer crashed down on the back of his skull and he pitched forward into blackness.

His head ached with a savage agony,

pain lancing through into his brain as he pushed himself up with a tremendous effort from his prone position on the hard, needle-edged rocks. When he raised his eyelids, it seemed to be still dark but as he rolled over on to his side, he saw the faint light that diffused the eastern sky, paling over the mesa in the far distance. He was weaker than a half-drowned kitten and every breath he took shocked pain back into his chest and lungs. Worse than his physical misery was the mental agony which came as memory flooded back into his mind. He recalled how the man he had thought had befriended him had suddenly turned on him in black treachery and held him up at gun point, relieving him of the map and silver he had been carrying.

Gradually, all of his senses came back to him. He wiped the back of his hand over his forehead. Blood had trickled there from the side of his head, congealing on his skin. It felt cold and encrusted on his flesh and a little shiver went through him as he tried to sit up. Sickness washed in a wave of nausea through his belly and it was all he could do to prevent it from overwhelming him.

Nursing his skull in both hands, he rocked back and forth on his knees, waiting for the rocks to steady their dizzying can-can in front of his pained vision. Gradually, he distinguished the trail to one side, running off through the high walls of the rocky canyon and he realized with a sudden shock that the horse he had been riding was no longer there. The man must have taken it when he had ridden off after knocking him out with that small, but deadly, Derringer pistol.

The sudden realization hit him with the force of a physical blow. Evidently the other had not meant him to follow his trail too closely, but why had he not killed him while he had had the chance? Surely he must have known that once he recovered, he would head after him, not stopping until he had tracked him down and exacted retribution. He mastered another spasm of nausea in a savage refusal to let it get the better of him. Other things around him resolved themselves out of the general overall haze, the bloody glimmer that danced and spun in front of his vision. The pale wash of the dawn on the edge of the world, the flatness of the sandy mesa that stretched away to the south as far as the eye could see, and to the north, to the cluster of buildings of the town, almost a mile away.

In the pale dawn light, he could make out the main street of the town, glimmering a little in the half light. There seemed to be little life there and he suddenly recalled the men who had been hunting him down through the town the previous evening when that man had stepped in and offered to help him slip out.

Then he saw something that shocked life back into his body, sent him crawling down the rocks, scrabbling for his gunbelt. If that little sidewinder had taken that —

He found it where it had fallen. Swiftly, ignoring the pain in his body and the dull, endless throbbing in his temples, he pulled the gunbelt on, buckled it swiftly, pulled out the guns and glanced down at them, spinning the chambers swiftly to make sure they were all loaded. Then, pulling himself together with an effort, he levered his bruised body back up among the rocks and peered through the growing dawn light at the trail which led back to the town. The bunch of riders were stirring up the dust as they headed out of town heading in his direction. He did not have to see them to know who they were. Jess Durman and his boys, riding back to the ranch after a long and fruitless night trying to pin him down. By now, they must know that he had slipped through their fingers.

Crouched among the cold rocks, he watched them come on. They pushed their mounts at a cruel, punishing pace and ahead of them rode the big man himself, Jess Durman, a man who had sworn to kill him, not for killing his two best men, but for refusing to work for him at whatever his game might be.

At the point where the trail forked, he saw them pause. Durman lifted a hand as he twisted a little in the saddle, then waved his arm in the direction of the rocks. A brief yell came from him as he urged his horse forward, the men tailing along behind him in single file. There was little time to be lost if he did not want to be discovered.

Another five minutes and that bunch of killers would be on him. Sweat dripping from his forehead, the palms of his hands suddenly greasy, he crawled through the sharp-edged rocks, feeling them cut through his clothing and into his hands and knees until they were raw flesh.

Raw, red, naked and barren, the rocks piled high on each other as he moved as far as he could from the trail. In the distance, he picked out the steady drumming of horses moving upgrade and urgency forced him on.

His breath came rasping into his throat, burning in his mouth.

The head of the oncoming column was a vague motion around the bend in the canyon trail. Clint thrust his body hard among the rocks, pulling down his head. Now the men were dead on him, only a few yards away, already slackening speed until the nearest rider was almost within arm's reach of where he lay.

Someone said harshly: 'You reckon he must've headed this way?'

'Well he wasn't anywhere in town,' said Durman from the head of the column. 'He must've headed out along one of the trails and a hunted man doesn't take the trail across the mesa, tracks show up too well in the dust. He'll have come this way for sure. Burns may have spotted him. Dismount and take a look around.'

Clint found himself boxed in now, unable to move without being seen. He lay absolutely still, scarcely daring to breathe, knowing that even with his guns in his hands, he could not possibly take on this bunch with any sort of chance at all. He heard the men climbing down from their saddles and moving around, boots striking the hard rocks underfoot, but he dared not lift his head to see what they were doing.

Gently, he eased his legs from under him, tried to slither an inch at a time further from the trail. The milling horses were making so much noise now that he doubted if anyone would hear his slight movements. Then a man from a little distance further along the trail yelled full and loud.

'What is it?' called Durman from somewhere nearer at hand. 'Have you found that *hombre*?'

'It's Burns,' called a harsh voice. 'Somebody got him plumb centre, I reckon.'

'Hell,' swore Durman. Clint could hear him moving along the trail. There was a pause, then the cattleman said harshly. 'Reckon this proves he came along this trail. He must've spotted

Burns some distance away otherwise he'd never have got close enough to pull anything like this.'

There was the scrape of a match, then Durman said sombrely. 'He's dead, all right.'

'Maybe we ought to have left a couple of men,' said another voice.

'Can't be helped now. Burns has paid the price of being stupid and not keeping his eyes open with a man like this gunslick around.'

'Do we keep right on after him?' queried a fresh voice, 'There are tracks here. Looks like two horses.'

'Two men.' There was a note of surprise in Durman's tone now. 'You sure?'

'Take a look-see for yourself.'

'He's right,' said a man harshly. 'Two men riding together. One of 'em stopped here and the other must've circled around Burns and dropped him without much warning. He got off one shot from this rifle.'

Very carefully, Clint edged back

another couple of yards until he found himself in a broad cleft in the rocks, He lifted his head with a slow stealth and peered down on to the trail almost immediately below him. There was a small bunch of men milling around in the narrow canyon, and two men standing close to Durman, staring down at the inert body of the guard Clint had shot earlier that night. One of the men had the other's rifle in his hands, had evidently been examining it closely.

As yet they did not suspect his presence there. The fact that his horse was gone added to their belief that he too had ridden out after killing the look-out man. They did not seem to consider it worthwhile to search the rocks on either side of the trail.

They remained there while his leg muscles twisted and knotted into a painful cramp and it was all he could do to stop himself from crying out with the agony. Some of the men were muttering among themselves, evidently wanting to be on the move again, believing that they would find no other sign of him there, reckoning that he was probably many miles away and still travelling.

Then Durman said impatiently. 'We're wastin' time, men. Let's move out. My guess is that he's headed south and he won't stop runnin' until he's clear through Mexico.'

They moved back, swung up into the saddles, paused for a moment peering about them at the rocky wilderness in the pale dawn light, then touched spurs to their mounts and rode out quickly, moving upgrade still, passing out of his sight around one of the sharply-angled bends in the trail. Clint lay quite still and listened to the steady abrasion of their movement on the rocky trail, waited until it had grown small in the distance, before moving his cramped legs, sucking in his breath with a sharp gasp as the pain stabbed briefly through his body. He reached a sitting position and contemplated his present situation.

He had no horse and it was at least a mile back to town along that open stretch of trail. From what he had seen of the men riding with Durman, the rancher had not considered it necessary to leave a group of men in town to watch out for him. There had been almost the same number of men with him then as he had noticed when they had ridden into town the previous day.

With an effort, he pushed himself to his feet, hung for a moment with his hands braced against the cold rock in order to hold himself up, then managed to get on his feet and stay there. There was a dizziness in his mind, but he managed to retain a tight grip on himself, edging down to the trail, stumbling occasionally on the treacherous rocks. He thought once more of the man who had robbed him and the dark anger came rising in him again, wiping away most of the pain and weariness in his desire to find that man again.

The dawn had brightened sufficiently now for him to see most of the details around him, but his vision kept blurring now and again and he was forced to halt on several occasions, spreading his legs wide, bracing himself to stay upright. The sun had lifted before he cleared the rocky ledges, throwing its glaring fight over the scene around him, lifting the heat head. He half fell down the last few feet to the trail, scarcely caring now whether or not those men with Durman had left the scene or were circling around to try to pick him up still.

The trail back into town was old and well used, but there was no one on it that morning at sun-up. It stretched away in front of him, empty and deserted, a pale ribbon of hard ground amid the shifting sands which lay in an endless sea on either side of it, blurring and wavering in front of his vision. He started back on the long journey to the town.

His legs slipped and swayed under him, knees faltering under his weight. He would have liked nothing better than to lie down and close his eyes in sleep, to surrender to the terrible bone-aching fatigue that dwelt in him, but a grim doggedness forced him on, enabled him to find those last reserves of strength which carried him along the trail. To his sickness-blurred vision, it seemed that the town receded in front of him and time stretched itself out into long, individual eternities of agony, breath rasping into his sandpaper throat, burning like fire in his lungs, paining his chest. Grit worked its way under his eyelids, lined his face with a mask of yellow.

The sun worked its way up into the cloudless heavens, a glaring disc of fire that burned all of the colour from the sky around it, reflected itself in dizzying waves from the mesa. Hunger gnawed at his belly and thirst tightened the constricting muscles of his throat, making it difficult to swallow whenever he tried to rid himself of the foul taste in his mouth.

At length, he was forced to rest up in

a small hollow a little way off the trail. The heat head was reaching a piled-up intensity. This day was now more punishing to him than before, every single breath a labour, eyes screwed up tight in his head in an effort to relieve the pounding glare. In spite of his determination to stay awake, he slipped into a half-doze, wakened as a sudden sound cut down through his consciousness, every nerve in him strung tight.

He lay absolutely still, not moving a single muscle, yet completely alert and wide-awake. Here, in the hollow, he was out of sight of anyone riding the trail. For a moment, the sounds that filtered to him made little sense, all jumbled and blurred together. Then he lifted his head gently and peered through the blinding sun-haze that shone full on his face. Screwing his eyes up to mere slits, he made out the small group of figures less than thirty yards from his position, the small, stoop-shouldered, bewhiskered man who stood with the packhorse and mule strung along behind; and the two men seated on horseback, rifles in their hands, their cruel faces edged with shadow under the large-brimmed hats they wore.

Clint grinned thinly as he moved forward, shifting his body slightly, easing the Colts from their holsters, checking briefly that he had reloaded every chamber and then sliding forward, legs under him.

The harsh voices of the men drifted across to him. 'Now just act sensible, old-timer and you won't get hurt.'

'Why you ornery side-winders,' growled the other hoarsely. 'I'll be damned if I'll let you get away with this.' He moved his right hand a little.

The taller of the two men snapped thinly: 'You'll be dead if you make a stupid move like that, mister. Now shuck that gunbelt and move away from that horse. Reckon you've got silver a-plenty there.'

'Why you — you . . . ' For a moment, it seemed the other was going to risk pulling the gun, even with the two rifles lined up on him. Then he shrugged in bitter defeat and it was at that moment that Clint decided to take a hand.

He rose up from the sand like a ghost from the grave, Colts held in his hands. His voice was thin as he called: 'Hold it there, fellas.'

The men whirled in unison. For a second, all motion seemed to have been cut off as if their limbs had become frozen. Clint stepped out of the hollow and it must have seemed to the outlaws that he took his eyes off them momentarily, but in the same instant that he half-turned, Clint swung back sharply, his gaze drilling into the others, the guns in his hands levelling swiftly, too quickly for the eye to follow. Caught as they tried to bring their rifles to bear, the men gave a sharp yell of defiance. The shots roared tremendously in the clinging silence. The impact of Clint's slugs knocked both men back from their saddles, sent them spinning to the ground. One was dead before he hit the sand. The other, badly wounded, still tried to squirm around and level his rifle at the man who strode forward. Clint fired again, his bullet taking the other clear between the eyes and he flopped back under the rearing hoofs of his horse as it pawed at the air in terror.

A vibrant hush followed. Nothing moved except for the slight coil of blue smoke that lifted from Clint's gun. The old prospector turned and stared at him in surprise, then opened his mouth into a toothy grin.

'Reckon you came along just in time, mister,' he said tightly. 'Figgered I was done for there.' He glanced around in surprise. 'But where in hell did you pop up from?'

'Back there a piece,' Clint said. He holstered the guns, walked over to the two bodies lying on the ground. He said: 'You know either of these men?'

'Nope.' The other shook his grizzled head. 'Ain't seen either of 'em around before. Must be new in these parts, maybe drifters movin' down from the north, hopin' to get rich quick and then head out over the mesa.'

He rubbed at the whiskers on his chin, eyes bright with contemplation. 'You look as if you've been in a spot o' trouble too, mister.'

'That's right,' Clint nodded. 'I had Durman on my tail back in town and accepted the help of somebody who said he'd help me get away. He held me up and took somethin' valuable.'

'This trail is full of side-winders, mister.' The other's brow puckered. 'But I want to thank you for buying in back there.' He proffered his hand and Clint grasped it, feeling the firm strength that was in the work-calloused fingers. The oldster's hands were frank and full of gratitude.

'The name's Cleve Merriam. I have a little mine up in the hills, fifteen miles back. First time I've been stopped on the trail into town, but it's a common thing now. Plenty of the others have been held up and robbed of their silver even before they can be robbed in the saloons.'

'My name's Clint Lanner.' He nodded. 'I gathered those fellas were goin' to grab off everythin' you'd got.'

'You'd have found a finished man if you'd happened along any later,' grinned the other. He nodded his head towards the two mounts. 'Care to stretch your luck a little further and ride on into town with me? You can get one of them horses. Reckon they won't be needin' 'em any longer. I'd like to repay you for what you did.'

'Thanks, Merriam,' Clint gave a quick nod. He had already figured on riding into town. Moving over, he swung up into the saddle on one of them, letting the other drift along behind. There might be questions asked in town by Sheriff Burnham but with this man's testimony he knew there would be little to fear from that. Even the sheriff had admitted that outlaws roamed these trails looking for the miners, robbing them of their silver.

With another look over the empty land behind them, they rode on towards the town, shimmering in the heat haze. Merriam took the lead and Clint rode slowly behind him, busy with his thoughts, trying to figure things out. Would Durman have a man back in town, just to keep an eye open in case he did ride back? It seemed more than possible, it was highly probable. He thought back to the man in the black frock coat and the line of his jaw hardened. It was just possible that Merriam might be able to help him here. As a silver prospector, he would know most of the places in this territory, might be able to identify some of the places which had been marked in on that scrap of tattered paper. If he could, Clint felt reasonably certain that he might be able to recall sufficient of the map itself to take himself there. He doubted if the thief would take anyone else into his confidence, at least not until he had ridden out there himself and looked the place over, satisfying himself as to the authenticity of the map.

A half hour's ride brought them into the outskirts of town and now Clint felt his flesh begin to twitch a little and the tiny spot between his shoulder blades itched warningly. If Durman had left a man behind, it was unlikely that he would recognize him. It could be any of the men who walked along the boardwalk and eyed him with a curious glance, or lounged in the high-backed chairs, well back from the dusty road and in the shade of the buildings on either side. They reined up in front of the sheriff's office.

'You figure on goin' in there and tellin' Burnham what happened?' queried Merriam, eyeing him sharply.

'I reckon it would be the best thing to do. Somebody is goin' to find those two dead men back there soon, and pass word along to him. Besides, it might be that someone will recognize these horses.'

'Guess you're right,' nodded the other in grudging agreement. It was obvious from his remark and attitude that he had little respect for Burnham. The shadow had come back to the other's face. 'Better watch Burnham,' he said quietly, as Clint slid from the saddle. 'He's a real tricky one. Whether he's in with Durman or not, I don't know. But he could be and if he is, then he'll pass word back to him sure as shootin'.'

'I'll be careful.' Clint nodded. He tethered the two horses to the rail, stepped up on to the boardwalk, then pushed open the door of the office and went inside.

Sheriff Burnham was seated behind his desk, legs up on top of it, leaning back in his chair, a black cigar between his lips. He had the look of a man without a single care in the world, as if all of his troubles were being taken care of by someone else. He stared openmouthed at Clint as the other strode in, then swung his feet abruptly from the desk and sat bolt upright in his chair, the cigar almost falling from his lips.

'Lanner!' He spoke the single word in

a hoarse tone. 'I thought you were — '

'Dead?' murmured Clint softly, 'or maybe run out of the territory by Durman and his hoodlums?' He shook his head slowly, grinning broadly, viciously. 'I'm afraid you would be wrong on both counts, Sheriff. As you can see, I'm here and I've got some trouble to drop into your lap.'

The other regained his composure with an effort, then his eyes narrowed and he said tartly. 'What sort of trouble, Lanner? I thought I warned you what would happen if you started stirring things up in town.' He half-rose to his feet, then sank back in his chair as Clint advanced on the desk and towered over him, leaning forward and resting his weight on his arms, lowering his head until his face was only a few inches from the other's. He saw the man strain back away from him, noticed the tiny beads of sweat that suddenly popped out on the sheriff's features and began to trickle down his forehead.

'This trouble was none of my makin',

Sheriff,' he snapped. 'A couple of outlaws tried to hold up an old prospector, named Merriam, on his way into town. Fortunately for him, I happened along and those two *hombres* tried to go for their rifles. You'll find 'em both stretched out on the sand about a mile from town if you care to go out to bring 'em in. I figure they won't be goin' no place so you can take your time about this chore.'

'Now don't be perky with me, Lanner,' blustered the other, trying to regain a little of his dignity. 'I'm still the sheriff around here and if there's any investigatin' to do, then I'll do it. Just you remember that.'

Clint grinned again, but there was no mirth in the smile and none of it touched his eyes. He straightened up. 'Suit youself, Sheriff,' he said, almost too casually. 'But Merriam is outside now, if you want to question him about the shootin'.'

'I'll get around to that if I reckon it's necessary,' grunted Burnham. He chewed around the cigar between his lips, then got heavily to his feet and riffled through the papers on his desk with fingers that were not quite steady. When he looked up again, he said, 'You figurin' on stayin' in town this time? Didn't see any sign of you last night when Durman and his boys were on the hunt for you. Figured you'd done the wisest thing and skipped town.'

'Maybe Durman and his men may be less cute than they figure,' Clint said, his tone giving nothing away. 'I'll be over in the saloon if you want me any more, with my friend, Merriam.'

Burnham moved around the side of the desk, hitched his gunbelt a little higher about his middle. Speaking around the cigar clamped firmly between his teeth now, he said: 'Let me give you a word of advice, mister. This town is no paradise, I'll admit that. But I can usually keep it under control, except for a handful of boisterous cowboys who like to whoop things up on pay night. But you seem intent on bustin' the place wide open, and for some reason known only to yourself. What's ridin' you I don't know, but I figure you'd better keep it to yourself.'

'I'll remember your words, Sheriff,' murmured Clint quietly. 'Like I said before, I don't come here lookin' for trouble, but I won't run away from it if it comes lookin' for me.'

He went out into the street, nodded up to Merriam, then swung up into the saddle of one of the horses leaving the other tethered to the rail. At the livery stables, they watered and grained the horses and the mule, putting the latter into a stall well away from the horses. Then they went along to the saloon. As he walked, moving warily in the bright sunlight, Clint kept his eyes open for any sign of trouble. He knew that if Durman had left orders that he was to be shot down on sight if he ever showed up in town again, that death could come with a surprising suddenness and from any direction.

Even at that early hour of the day,

there were card games in progress in the saloon. A man with a bowler hat sat at the piano and ran his fingers over the keys with an almost absent air, plucking melodies from the strings of the ancient instrument as though by magic. Going over to the bar, Clint motioned for a bottle and when the bartender brought it, he poured drinks for Merriam and himself. Merriam set a small bag on the bar and the man in the white apron picked it up, opened it and squinted suspiciously inside, poured a little of it into the palm of his hand and stared down at the grains, then gave a quick nod of satisfaction and weighed the bag experimentally in his hand.

Clint dug into his pocket for some coin, but the other, seeing the movement pushed his hand away.

'I owe you for this, Lanner,' he said quietly. 'I made a good strike up there in the hills and if you hadn't happened along, I'd have lost the lot.'

Clint shrugged. He drank his whisky, looking at the array of bottles at the back of the bar, admiring the way in which the bartender worked, seeming to know exactly where to go for any drink that was called for. With a part of his mind, he listened to the ebb and flow of conversation in the saloon. The man next to him said quietly. 'Let's get ourselves a table. I've got some jawin' to do.'

'Sure,' Clint nodded. He also wanted to talk with the other, feeling that here was a man he could trust in this town where everyone could be a crook.

They found a table set well apart from the others. For the time being, no one seemed to be taking any notice of them. The poker games were still in progress at the far side of the saloon and the small bunch of men who leaned against the bar appeared to be more interested in the card games than in them. Merriam slumped down in his chair, set the full bottle of whisky on the table in front of them, poured a drink into each of the glasses, then eyed Clint over the rim of his own before drinking it down. He wiped his mouth with the back of his gnarled hand.

'You don't look like the ordinary cut of men in this town,' he said, leaning forward and speaking in a low husky tone. 'I figure you're here for some other reason.' His gaze was shrewd and Clint knew that as far as the other was concerned, this was not the whisky talking. In spite of his earlier assessment of the man, he still wondered how far he could really trust him.

He eventually decided to take a chance. He needed information if he was to locate the mine shown on that piece of paper and the sooner he reached that spot and took a quick look-see for himself, the sooner he would catch up with the man who had robbed him. The thought of the other sent a fresh wave of anger running through his mind, anger directed not only at the thief, but at himself for having been so stupid as to have allowed it to happen.

Carefully, he asked: 'You ever heard

of a place called Broken Horse Pass?'

The other ran the name over in his mind for a moment and then gave a quick nod. 'Sure,' he said harshly. 'It's way out of town, best part of thirty miles from here, I reckon. Well off the beaten track. What interest you got in that god-forsaken spot anyway, Lanner?'

'Plenty,' Clint rubbed his chin thoughtfully, then went on, picking his words with care. 'You ever hear of a strike called the El Dorado Mine?'

The old prospector stared at him, eyes widened just a shade. There was a look of hard disbelief on his grizzled features. 'You ain't believin' in that ghost bonanza, are you?' he said finally.

Clint forced a quick smile. 'That's the sort of reaction I got from most everybody I've talked to about this place,' he said quietly. 'But I changed my mind about whether this strike exists or not when I was robbed of the map and a nugget of silver as big as your finger that must've come from there.'

'Now how can you be so sure that map wasn't just a forgery? There was talk a while back of the El Dorado Mine. Folk reckoned it was up in that territory near Broken Horse Pass right enough,' he went on musingly. 'But so many men have gone out lookin' for it since it was discovered and nobody has ever come within sight of it. Not only that, but plenty have died up there in that country.'

'Does the name of Everett mean anythin' to you?' Clint asked, very softly.

He saw from the faint gust of expression that swept over the other's face that it did. The man nodded his head slowly, soberly now. 'You ever meet Everett?'

Clint nodded. 'I met him, but only for a little while. He was dyin' when I found him out in the desert several days' ride north of here. He'd been ambushed and shot down by a group of men who must've been followin' him, waitin' to get their hands on that map.

But they never found it. He'd got it tucked away inside his boot, gave it to me just before he died.'

'Then you could be right.' There was a fresh break of interest in the other's voice now, showing through on to his face. A moment later, the sudden gleam in his eyes clouded. He sank back in his chair, staring down at the empty glass in his fingers. 'But you ain't got the map any longer. That's right, ain't it?'

'That's right,' Clint nodded. 'But I memorized it enough to get me there if I can find this Broken Horse Pass.'

'Now you're talkin'.' Merriam's eyes moved to the men at the other end of the bar, then swung back to Clint. 'Why're you tellin' me all this, mister?'

'I need help. I need somebody who can guide me to this place and who can be trusted. You'll have a half share in anythin' we find there. Is it a deal?'

'You must be crazy givin' away silver like that, Lanner,' said the other quickly; then he stuck out his hand over the table. 'But if you're willin' to have it that way, then count me in.'

Clint poured a couple of drinks. 'Let's drink to our success,' he said quietly. 'But I figure I ought to warn you. That man who stole the map from me. He won't be hangin' around these parts. He'll have headed out there right now and he may try to stake a claim to that place.'

The other's eyes assumed a speculative look. 'I'm reckonin' that he won't know those parts too well,' he said soberly. 'If he merely rode out like you said, without plenty of grub and supplies, he'll probably die of thirst or starvation before he gets more'n a handful of silver from that strike. It's deadly country up there. No water unless you know where to look for it and in places, you can scarcely take a horse through. That's why I always take Betsy along whenever I go out. She comes in mighty handy.'

'Betsy,' said Clint, glancing up.

'The mule,' Merriam grinned toothily. He ruffled his beard. 'She can get through where even a man would be lost. A mite stubborn, but I wouldn't part with her for all that.'

'When can you be ready to move out?' Clint asked. He tried to hide the urgent impatience in his mind. The thought of that thief, somewhere to the south, getting his hands on all of that silver, made him angry. It wasn't so much that he wanted it for himself. Wealth like that seldom brought a man happiness, but Everett had died with a gunman's bullet in him just because of that map and he felt he had a part to play to ensure that no other thief got his hands on even a grain of that silver. He hoped that Merriam was right about the kind of country in that neighbourhood. If he was, then there was a real chance they might be able to make up some of this lost time. Certainly it hadn't seemed to him that the man who had robbed him had been anything of a miner and it was doubtful if he would have taken even the most elementary precautions.

Glancing up at him across the table, Merriam said. 'I reckon you'd better get some sleep, Lanner, before we move out. You won't get much comfort on this trail and a good night's rest always helps. I found that out the hard way in the fifteen years I've been prospectin' in these parts. Besides, we can't move out without gettin' plenty of provisions. I'll get them this afternoon. You'd better cut across to the hotel and get yourself some shut-eye.'

'Maybe you're right,' Clint gave a brief nod. He began to realize just how weary he really was and that vicious crack on the back of the skull had not helped his physical condition.

At the hotel, the clerk gave him a sleepy glance. It was almost high noon, and in this town it was the time for siesta, particularly among the Mexican population. But the sleepiness vanished abruptly as soon as he saw who it was who stood in front of the desk.

'Why, *Señor* Lanner. We thought that you were — '

He broke off helplessly, not sure of what to say. His mouth hung open slackly as Clint reached out for the key, to his room. He did not answer at first as Clint asked: 'My gear still up in my room?'

Then he swallowed thickly, nodded his head rapidly several times. 'Of course. Nothing has been touched. We did not know if you would return, when we heard that *Señor* Durman was looking for you in the streets.'

'Now you know that I have returned,' Clint retorted. His weariness edged his tone with more anger than he had intended. He took his key, climbed the stairs and went into his room, locking the door at his back. As the clerk had said, nothing here had been touched. He had half anticipated that someone might have come in to search the place, figuring that he would never return once Durman had set his gunhawks after him in the streets of the town.

For a moment, he paused at the window, looking down into the street.

He saw the swing doors of the saloon open and a bunch of drunks stagger out. One of them fell into the middle of the dusty street and the others set up a raucous laughter. No one made any attempt to help him back on to his feet again. He washed his face, rubbed some of the dried blood from his head, then sat down on the edge of the low bed, feet thrust out straight in front of him. Since he had ridden into this town, he seemed to have done little but wash bumps on his skull. Grimacing wryly, he pulled off his jacket and shirt, checked that there was no one outside on the balcony, then thrust a gun under his pillow, stretched himself out on the bed, feeling the refreshing coolness of the sheets against his tired, bruised body. Merriam had been right in one respect, he thought tiredly. He certainly could do with one long sleep, free from any interruptions.

★ ★ ★

172

He did sleep. For how long, he wasn't sure, but when he finally woke, the sunlight was still streaming in through the unshuttered windows. It was not until he pushed himself upright and stared about him more clearly that he noticed the sun was somewhere in the eastern half of the sky whereas when he had fallen asleep it had been just past its zenith, riding down the long slide to the western horizon. He must have slept almost round the clock, his weariness had been so great, so overpowering.

Thrusting his legs to the floor, he got up, rubbed the stubble on his chin, then moved across to the window, peering out. The sun had just begun to clear the horizon, far out to the east, throwing long slanting shadows over the street down below. Washing, he shaved and felt better than he had for several days. The sleep had done him a power of good, he mused, eased the pain and ache from his limbs, clearing his mind. There was still a faint, throbbing agony in his head if he moved it quickly, but that would go away.

He pulled on his shirt after knocking most of the dry dust from it, then his gunbelt and jacket. Swiftly, he made up the saddle-roll, tightened the leather thongs around it. He would not be riding back to this hotel in quite a spell if everything went all right with the old prospector.

The question now was: where was Merriam? Likely he had a place in town where he could bunk down whenever he rode in with his hard-earned silver, before he started out on the trail once more, out to win more of the precious white metal from the ground, only to lose it in a few nights, either by having it taken by force, or by cheating at cards. Either way, he would soon lose it and would philosophically ride out to get more. It wasn't likely that the outlaws who infested this part of the territory would stop or even trail a man riding out of town, back into the inhospitable hills. They much preferred the easier way of taking the silver once it had been won from the hard ground. They weren't interested in staking claims to the silver strikes whenever they were made in the hills, although the same might not be said for a man such as Jess Durman. It was just possible that he might have a man trailed if there was word of a rich strike having been made in the territory. Once he owned the land on which the strike had been made, he could get men to dig for him.

His first place of call was the saloon. The bartender was just setting the glasses up on the counter, gave him a sharp, bright stare. At that time of the morning, there was no one in the bar. Only a swamper with a broom sweeping out the debris from the previous night, moved slowly with a shuffling gait around the tables.

'You seen anythin' of that fella who was with me last night?' Clint asked of the bartender.

The other shook his head. 'Merriam?

He left about two hours after you did. Was pretty drunk when he finally went. I guess he went over to his usual place to sleep it off.'

'Where might that be?'

'Down the street a couple of blocks, then turn right. Third shack along on the left. You can't miss it. Most of these old fellas go there whenever they hit town for a spendin' spree. You'll see plenty of 'em around.'

'Thanks,' Clint turned swiftly on his heel and walked out. He made his way quickly along the boardwalk.

There were few people out. A couple of riders in the distance spurred their mounts out of town, taking the north trail. He gave them only a brief, cursory glance, then moved off the main street down the narrower road that led off at right angles to it, soon located the long, low-roofed building with the faded sign hanging outside the door, the wooden, painted board swinging slightly in the cool morning breeze.

Inside, on several cots, a variety of

men were still sleeping. Clint let his gaze wander intently over them, searching for Merriam, but not seeing him there. For the first time, he felt a tiny imp of suspicion gnawing at his mind, nibbling away at the edges of his brain. If the other was not here, where could he be? Had something happened to the old fellow? Burnham knew he had ridden in with him, and the Sheriff might have passed that word on to someone else. There seemed to be plenty of people in town and around it, who were mighty interested both in him, and any friends he might have. It could be that some of them had decided to check on Merriam as the less dangerous of the two. If that was the case, he could be anywhere, always assuming he was still alive.

There was a sudden movement in the doorway at his back and he whirled quickly, staring through narrowed eyes at the man who came in. He was of middle age, greying at the temples, with a seamed face, although his eyes were still bright and polished.

'Lookin' for somebody, mister?' he asked. His tone was quiet but without real friendliness.

'I'm lookin' for a friend of mine,' Clint told him, noticing that the other did not carry any guns that could be seen. 'Cleve Merriam.'

'Is he in town?' The other sounded genuinely surprised. 'I ain't seen him for a while, must be more'n five months. He always heads for here when he does arrive. You sure he's here?'

'I came in with him yesterday mornin'. A couple of outlaws tried to hold him up outside of town. I left him in the saloon around midday. The bartender tells me he left a couple of hours later, figures he was headed here.'

The other's face bore a serious expression. 'He certainly never got here,' he said.

Clint stood there with his head bent a little, troubled at what might have happened to the old man. The men lying on the cots, some of them awake now, were in various attitudes, peering up at him through sleep-filled eyes. He knew that the man standing in front of him was telling the truth. There was that much in his voice and he did not seem the kind of man who wanted anything from these prospectors.

'You know where he might have gone after leaving the saloon?'

The man shook his head, the light through the open doorway glinting on his silvery hair. 'Reckon he might be any place in town. You figuring on lookin' for him? Could take you a long while. Is he that important to you?'

'He could be,' Clint said simply. 'I have to find him wherever he might be.'

There was nothing more to be gained there, Clint realized. Leaving the place, he headed along the street, figuring that perhaps, if Merriam had been too drunk really to know what he was doing, instinct might have sent him headed in this direction, but he had failed to reach that place. Right now, he might be sleeping off his drunken stupor behind some shack, his body huddled up for warmth from the cold of the night air.

There was no sign of the old man in that street and Clint moved on, into a narrower alley that led off from it, a rubbish-filled passage between two rows of low houses that backed on to it. In the hot sunlight, the smell of rotting garbage stung his nostrils and got into his throat, but he forced himself to ignore it. He was on the point of moving on, past the mouth of the alley when he noticed something which made him pause. He went forward slowly, one hand hovering close to the butt of his gun. Rounding a stretch of rotten, wooden fencing, he saw the figure lying inertly on the ground, almost completely out of sight so that it would have been easy to have missed him. The man lay on his face but Clint did not need a second glance to tell who it was. Gently, he rolled the other over, felt for the pulse. It still beat strongly in the skinny wrist and he let a sigh of relief go from his nostrils, at least the other was still alive. He glanced at the man's head and saw the lump which had been raised on the back of the skull. So Merriam had received the same kind of treatment as he had. Fortunately, the other had a thick skull or it might have been the end for him.

A few moments later, the other groaned, opened his eyes for a moment and then screwed them up again as the bright sunlight struck him.

'Take it easy, old-timer,' Clint said softly. 'You're all right now.'

'What in tarnation happened?' The other shook his head as though trying to remember, winced as pain lanced through his skull. 'I remember leavin' the saloon and headin' for Joe's and that's all.'

'I'd say you've been relieved of any silver you still had when you left the saloon,' Clint told him. 'They must've been tailin' you all the way, knocked you cold and dragged you down here where you wouldn't be found for some time.'

The other felt in his pockets, then nodded his head dolefully. 'Cleaned out. They took everythin' I had left.' His lips thinned. 'Why, I'll — '

'You'll do nothin',' Clint said sharply. 'Think you can stand if I give you a hand?'

He helped the other to his feet, holding him upright as the oldster swayed heavily against him. With an effort, Merriam pulled himself together. 'I'll be all right as soon as these hammers stop thumping inside my skull,' he said through tight lips. 'You got any idea who could've done this?'

'No,' Clint shook his head as he helped the other along the alley. 'It could've been any of those men in the saloon. They must all have seen the silver you were carryin'. Maybe even a chance word from that bartender.'

'Sure, sure,' said the other, a note of bitterness in his tone. 'I reckon you're right. But if we were to — '

Clint cut him off. 'There's more silver than you dreamed of at the El Dorado Mine,' he said tightly, 'or had you forgotten we were to head out there today?'

'Hell, I'd forgotten.' The other nodded, then forced a wide grin. 'But we need supplies.'

'I've still got somethin' left for supplies,' Clint released his hold on the other. 'Now let's get what we need and ride out. Seems to me this town is crawlin' with coyotes ready for our blood.'

In the main street, a few curious glances were thrown in Merriam's direction and the storekeeper glanced at the bruises on the prospector's face, but said nothing until he had made up their supplies, stacking them all neatly on the counter. Then he murmured, 'You fixin' to ride with this *hombre*, Merriam?'

'That's right,' retorted the old-timer harshly. 'Got any objections, Bob?'

'Not if you haven't,' replied the other, giving Clint a stiff-eyed jolt of a glance.

'Though I reckon you should know who he is.'

'And just who do you reckon I am?' Clint asked tautly. He saw the man flush a little under his tone. 'They reckon that you shot down two of Durman's men in the cantina,' said the other defensively. He stood well away from the counter, his eyes bright but wary, as if he expected Clint to go for his gun at any moment and start more gunplay in the store.

'Those two men called me out and drew on me first,' Clint retorted. 'You got anythin' against shootin' in self-defence?'

'Not a thing,' said the other, licking his lips a little, sure now that this conversation was getting a little out of hand and clearly wishing that he had not started it. 'Only Durman sure is set to bust up this town. We rely a lot on his custom and that of his men and if — '

'I get it now,' Clint said sharply. 'You're afraid that you'll lose custom and money. That's all you're really concerned about.'

'We all got our living to make,' said the other, his tone stubborn.

'Reckon we'd better take our supplies and get out of here,' said Merriam. He gathered up some of the sacks of food and started for the door.

5

Bonanza Trail

They rode south beyond the town and took the *arriero* trail which began a gradual ascent through the rocks and out into more open country. By high noon, they were well out of the rocks, riding slowly over the wide mesa where the glaring sunlight struck fire from the metal pieces of their bridles, sent painful flashes into their eyes. They kept to the trail here, watching for tracks and as he rode, Clint found himself speculating idly on the number of wanted men who must be hiding in this cruel, forbidding land, always on the run from the law, living in seclusion unless they were able to get themselves on to the payroll of some important and influential man like Jess Durman who would act as their protector against the law provided they did his bidding. The pinched-down mountains in the distance moved before them throughout the whole of that long, hot, sunlit afternoon. It was not until towards evening, when their shadows ran long and huge in front of them, that they seemed to be approaching the foothills and the horizon began to lift from the terrible, monotonous flatness of the mesa.

They made camp beside a small stream that came bubbling down from the hills, lighting a fire well back from the trail, in a small hollow surrounded by the tall trunks of the red pine which grew in profusion here. From the trail no one would see their fire and Clint felt reasonably safe here.

Clint smoked a cigarette in the flickering brilliance of the fire while the other put the bacon and beans on to cook over the fire. Merriam said: 'You see that trail we was followin' most of the way?'

'Sure,' Clint gave a brief, terse nod.

He stared down for a moment at the glowing red tip of the cigarette. 'I figure it must've been his. How far d'you reckon he is ahead of us?'

'Hard to say,' mused the other. He spooned the bacon and beans on to the two plates, held one out to Clint. 'He was hurryin' that mount of his. Don't make any mistake about that. I'd say he'll be there a day before we are.'

'Just what I figured,' Clint forced himself to keep the hard urgency from his voice. 'I know he had a partner when he attacked me the first time without getting his hands on the map. Could be he's decided to double-cross this *hombre* whoever he was. If not, then we'll have two of 'em to deal with when the time comes.'

'Plenty of places up there for a man to hide and watch the trail,' said Merriam, chewing on his food. 'It's a lonely place, nothin' but rocks and barrenness.'

'And you're sure you can find your way to Broken Horse Pass?'

The other nodded his head quickly. 'It's somethin' of a landmark along this trail. No difficulty gettin' there, but it's once we do reach the pass that we'll have to rely on your memory.' He eyed Clint with a bright-sharp stare as though wondering just how good that might be.

'How far to the pass?'

The other pursed his lips thoughtfully. 'With the mule, I figure we'll maybe get there sometime tomorrow afternoon. He'll have made better time unless he's pushed his horse too hard in those hills. Many a man has lost his life because his mount threw a shoe or went lame there.'

'I figure he'll know better than that,' Clint muttered. He sat back, just inside the circle of firelight, built himself a second smoke. He felt tensed and taut. The sun had gone down while they had been setting up their camp and now the stiff breeze that blew up from the mesa was cold and filled with tiny grains of sand, stinging their eyes. The thickening moon lifted from the eastern horizon with a yellow, silent majesty pushing its flaring silver light onward and downward, filtering through breaks in the leafy canopy overhead.

'Better bed down,' suggested Merriam, giving him a faint nod. 'We'll be makin' an early start in the morning.'

'You reckon we ought to take it in turn to keep watch?' Clint asked.

The other grinned. 'Ain't likely to be anybody movin' along this trail durin' the night. Besides, they won't see the fire through the trees.'

★   ★   ★

Clint pulled his blanket more tightly around him in an attempt to keep out the biting cold, slitting his eyes against the sand that came sweeping through the trees, lying on his back staring up at the bright stars which glittered brightly against the jet velvet of the sky. The sand on the trail would muffle the sound of any approaching riders, he realized and the thought troubled him. For a moment, he fancied he heard something in the distance, some sound which he could not identify and he lifted his head slowly from the blanket, straining his ears in attempt to pick it out more clearly. But after a few moments, he felt satisfied that there had been nothing more than the faint soughing of the wind in the lowermost branches of the pines and he lowered his head to the bedroll once more, glancing in Merriam's direction. The other was still asleep and no sound had penetrated into his consciousness.

It was possible he thought, turning events over in his mind as he lay in his blanket, unable to sleep, that the man who robbed him of the map was camped only a few miles away to the south-west. But even as the thought passed through his mind, he dismissed it as unlikely. The man would have ridden hell for leather along this trail, moving from one point to the next as given on that map, not stopping until he had reached the spot where the El Dorado Mine was supposed to be located.

One of the horses snickered quietly where it had been hobbled among the trees nearby, the sound jarringly loud in the clinging stillness of the small clearing and Clint rolled smoothly over on to his side, eyes wide open, straining to see into the yellow moonlight, to pick out anything that moved. The seconds and minutes ticked by with a monotonous slowness. There was something oddly weird and uncanny about this place at night, with the moon shining down with a ghostly yellow-white glow that touched everything so that the trees stood out like tall spectral fingers pointing to the sky.

Unable to content himself, he got up from his blankets, moved around the fire, skirting the pale glow from the feebly flickering flames in the centre of the clearing, and moved off into the trees to a spot where he would be able to overlook the trail. It was almost impossible to distinguish the trail from the sandy stretches of the mesa on either side of it and narrowing his eyes against the sudden glare of the moonlight as he stepped out of the fringe of trees, he looked up and down the trail in both directions. The moon was so bright that it was possible for him to see several miles along the trail, but nothing moved out there as he seated himself on an upthrusting boulder, the rifle held across his knees.

For close on an hour, he sat there, watching the trail, keen-eyed and alert in spite of the fact that he had had little sleep. Had he been mistaken when he had reckoned he had heard that far-off sound, almost like the drumming of hoofbeats along the trail, far in the distance? He was beginning to think that he must have been when he spotted the faint movement in the distance, at the very edge of his vision, a rising cloud of dust that moved with the rider. The other was too far away for him to make out any details clearly in the moonlight, but the rider was obviously headed along the trail in their direction and was coming up at a fast lick, spurring his mount more cruelly than was good for it. The man was in a big hurry and did not seem to be too cautious. Slowly, Clint lifted the rifle from his knees, moved back into the trees and roused Merriam. The old man mumbled softly, then came awake, staring about him, pushing himself up on to his arms.

'Rider comin' along the trail this way,' Clint said thinly. 'No noise now, until we see who it is and why he's in such a goshdarned hurry.'

'You reckon it could be somebody from town?' grunted Merriam. He stooped to pick up the ancient Sharps rifle, then hurried after Clint through the trees until they were overlooking the narrow winding trail. Crouching down in the shadows of the rocks, they watched the steady approach of the rider. Then, less than a quarter of a mile away, as the trail began to lift towards the trees, the other slowed his mount, checked the breakneck pace, and moved forward more carefully now. Occasionally, Clint saw him lean forward in the saddle, bending towards the ground, keeping his feet hooked tightly in the stirrups, obviously scanning the ground for sign of tracks. The sight heightened the feeling in Clint's mind that this man was no ordinary cowboy riding the trail, but a man with a very definite aim in mind, looking for someone, and the chances were that he could be searching for them.

While the other had been out there in the open, there would have been no need for caution on his part, but now he was approaching the high tree-covered ridges where a couple of men who had been on the trail for a long day, would have made camp.

A couple of hundred yards from where they crouched, the rider suddenly reined his mount, paused for a moment, casting his glance all about him, quartering the high slopes. Then he slithered from the saddle, reached up to jerk the rifle from its scabbard and moved away from the horse. Clint watched through narrowed eyes as he saw the man go down on one knee and examine the ground along the trail closely at that point. Realization came to him in a single instant and he sucked in his breath sharply, motioning Merriam to remain where he was, checking the old-timer as he made to lift the Sharps to his shoulder.

The other man knew that someone was likely to be watching the trail here and he was trying to pick out tracks to discover where they had left the main trail and ridden up into the trees. Tightening his lips into a thin, hard line, he whispered tautly to Merriam.

'Stay here and don't let him spot you. Whatever you do, don't try to use that rifle unless it's absolutely necessary. I want to take this *hombre* alive if I can and find out who he is and why he's trailin' us.'

'Much better to shoot him now and

have it done with,' said the other in a hoarse whisper. But he lowered the rifle and squatted down behind the rocks.

Peering through a crack between two knife-edged rocks, Clint saw that the man had moved off the track, was scuttling into the shadowed rocks on their side of the trail. Things were not going to be quite as simple as he had thought at first. Whoever the other was, he was an experienced frontiersman, knew how to read sign and it was improbable that he would move forward into a trap.

Clint cursed softly under his breath, motioned again to Merriam to stay where he was, then slithered snake-like into the mass of boulders that lay in front of him. The man was only guessing, but pretty soon he would begin to circle around, moving towards the rim of trees, knowing that if there was a camp hereabouts, that was where it was likely to be and he would try to sneak up on anyone there from behind, hoping to take them by surprise. The chances were he would not want to shoot anyone down until he was certain who they were.

Very carefully, Clint lifted his head, straining his eyes against the white glare of moonlight, striving to keep a close watch on the other as he moved further from the trail, deeper into the rocky ground immediately on the edge of the trees. Once the other was inside the timber, it would be virtually impossible to follow his movements except by ear and in the night, hearing was the most deceptive of the senses as he had discovered for himself on several occasions in the past.

Gently, he moved in the direction of the trees, reckoning that he was cutting across the other's trail, and that he would be close behind him as he moved into the timber. He felt his stomach muscles tighten into a hard knot and for long moments there was only silence all about him. Then, clearly, he heard the faint movement of the horses inside the ring of trees, guessed that they had picked up the presence of the gunman close by. Keeping his head and shoulders low, he slipped forward, gripping the Winchester tightly in his hands. There was nothing for it now but to stick close on the other's tail until the man made his move once he spotted the camp fire and the blankets stretched out close by.

An inch at a time, remaining more upright now that he was among the trees, he glided forward. The darkness, where the moonlight was unable to penetrate the thick covering of branches and leaves, was almost complete. From somewhere across the valley behind him, came the distant, dismal wail of a coyote and a little shiver went up and down Clint's spine. If only the other would make some sound or show himself for just a brief instant, it would be enough for him to pick out his position but clearly the gunman was taking no chances whatever. The pale gleam of the fireglow showed through the trees as he moved forward, searching with eyes and ears to try to find out if the man had made full circle around the clearing once he had spotted it and the camp fire, or whether he lay between the fire and himself. The Winchester was ready for use; he paused and held his breath until the only sound he could hear was the dull pounding of the blood in his ears. He had lived far too long with violence and danger not to feel a little afraid, but he did not allow this fear to rise up and take over control of him, to choke him as it might have done a lesser man. He held himself under tight control, knowing that when the time came this would be a personal showdown, that unless he played it right, it would be either himself or the other man.

Then, with a sudden abruptness that came with the shock of the unexpected, he heard the faint scrape of a boot against rock and held his head a little on one side as he strove to pinpoint the origin of the sound. It had been very faint and fleeting and in this dimness he could be sure of nothing. Then, a moment later, the sound came again, and he let his breath go in little pinches through his nostrils as he knew almost exactly where the man was. He had circled around the clearing, as Clint had guessed that he would, so as to come on it from the side furthest from the trail, thereby hoping to take anyone there utterly by surprise.

Such was his uncanny ability to place sound, that he could almost have fired the Winchester now, in the darkness, and hit the other, but he deliberately held his fire. If possible, he wanted to take this man alive. There were things he needed to know. If it was one of Durman's men, then it might mean that the rancher was still on his trail, still determined to kill him.

Keeping his body well into the shadows, far beyond the faint ring of firelight, he stiffened for a moment as he caught his first glimpse of the man. He was well back among the trees on the opposite side of the clearing, only visible when he made a slight movement. The man had spotted the horses tethered among the trees and was obviously a little unsure of the best thing to do in these circumstances. It was just possible that he had figured Clint to be alone on the trail and was surprised to see so many horses there. He seemed to be searching around for any sign of them, still cautious and alert. Then he moved forward to the edge of the clearing, the rifle balanced in his hands. Clint let him move another couple of feet, then stepped through the trees, Winchester trained on the other and said in a mild faintly derisive tone. 'Hold it there, mister and let that rifle drop.'

He clearly heard the sharp intake of breath as the other lifted his head suddenly and then turned slowly. He could make out the man's face as a pale blur in the fireglow as the man stood irresolute, not moving a muscle.

'That's better,' Clint moved out into the clearing. 'Just stay there or this rifle might go off. I've got quite an itchy trigger finger whenever anybody comes pussyfooting it up on me in the dark.'

He reached the other in a couple of strides, held the barrel of the rifle on the man's chest with one hand, bracing the stock against his thigh, as he reached out with the other hand, plucked the gun from the other's unresisting fingers and tossed it behind him into the brush. Stooping again, he relieved the man of his hand weapons, then ordered him out into the middle of the clearing.

A couple of seconds later, there was another movement and Merriam stepped through into the firelight. He gave the man a bright stare. 'I see you got him without any trouble, Clint,' he said harshly. 'Any idea who the critter is?'

'Not at the moment, but I figure he's goin' to tell us before long.'

'Just what sort of a stunt is this?' snapped the other savagely as he stared from Clint to the old prospector and then back again. He glared at Clint through slitted eyes. 'A hold-up? If it is, then you'll get mighty lean pickings from me I can tell you.'

'Don't try to bluff me,' Clint told him, backing off a couple of paces where he could keep an eye on the other. 'I'm in no mood for foolin' around. I know just who you are and what you're doin' here.'

'Yeah.' The other forced a thin-lipped grin, 'Suppose you tell me who I am, mister.' It was clear that the other still seemed intent on trying to bluff it out with them.

'Right, I'll tell you who I reckon you are,' he snapped. 'One of Jess Durman's men. He must've heard from Sheriff Burnham that I'd pulled out of town, headed in this direction. Just where are the rest of the bunch. Ridin' up close on your tail waitin' for your report?'

'You don't know what you're talkin' about,' said the other and there was something in his tone, some note of defiance that made Clint feel a little unsure of himself.

'Maybe you can think of somethin' better. Otherwise, why did you move off the trail back there after searching for sign, and come circling round, obviously hopin' to shoot us in the back?'

The other said nothing, but simply stood staring at him with an expression of sullen anger in his deep-set eyes and naked hatred in the set of his lips.

'You not goin' to talk?' Clint asked with a deceptive mildness.

The other grinned viciously. 'I'm tellin' you nothin,' he snarled. 'And there ain't no way you can make me either. You're not the kind of man who would shoot another down in cold blood without givin' him a chance to defend himself.'

'You reckon not,' Clint raised his brows a little. 'I don't take too kindly to coyotes sneakin' up on me and tryin' to take me by surprise. I figure you would have shot us both without givin' us an even break if the tables had been turned.'

'I'll make the critter talk for you, Clint,' Merriam edged his way forward, and there was an unholy glint in his eyes that Clint had not seen before. 'I spent a while with the Utes and they know a few tricks that'll make anybody talk. Just tell me what you want to know and I'll have it out of him before you know it.'

'What do you have to say to that, *hombre*?' Clint eyed the other closely. For a moment he was sure he noticed an expression of fear gust over the man's granite features, knew that Merriam's threat had struck home.

'Why, the old coot — ' snapped the outlaw.

'Easy now, sonny.' Merriam moved towards him, stepped by him as the other cringed away from him and went over to the fire, kicking it with the toe of his boot, sending the sparks showering redly into the sky, then piling fresh dry faggots on to it until it was blazing fiercely again. 'A red-hot brandin' iron applied to the right spot works wonders. If it don't then there are other ways which are guaranteed and — '

'Just keep that crazy old fool away from me,' yelled the other, hoarsely, really terrified now. Evidently, he knew that Merriam was not fooling this time, that he really could do what he said.

'You goin' to tell us who you are and why you were sneakin' up on us like that?'

'Sure, sure.' The other spoke so quickly that the words almost tumbled over themselves. There were beads of sweat shining on his forehead and rolling down the sides of the pinched nose. 'Only keep him away from me.'

'All right then — talk,' Clint snapped. 'You one of Durman's men?'

'No, I'm not.' The other muttered the words harshly, his eyes flicking nervously to where Merriam hunkered over the fire. 'Sure I've heard of Durman, but I'm not workin' for him, never have. And I didn't know it was you here, I thought it was — ' He broke off, lips tightening.

'Go on,' snapped Clint harshly. 'Just who did you reckon it was camping here?' He had the feeling that the other was lying, hoping to gain time. Maybe he was working for Durman, and he was trying to buy his life by stalling until the rest of the crew rode up.

In a sullen tone, the other said: 'Jeb Calton.'

Clint knit his brows in puzzlement, stared round for a moment at Merriam, but it was obvious that the name meant nothing to him.

'I reckon you'd better do some fast talkin', he said shortly. 'I'm fast losin' my patience. Who in tarnation is Jeb Calton? And why should you be sneakin' up on him like this?'

'He's a dirty, double-crossin' thief,' said the other harshly. There was no doubting the anger in his tone. 'Tricked me when he got his hands on that map you was carryin', pulled out of town without a word. I reckoned he must've taken this trail and I figured I might be able to catch up with him before he got to this El Dorado Mine.'

'So that's it,' Clint breathed. He knew now as the flood of realization washed over him at the other's words. Jeb Calton, the little man in the black frock-coat who had befriended him, only to turn against him and rob him of that map — and this man who stood in front of him now, must have been the one who had crept up behind him in the darkness of that alley when Calton had called to him, luring him forward.

'What do you reckon we ought to do with him?' Merriam asked, straightening up from the fire, guessing that his efforts were not going to be needed now.

'By rights, I reckon I ought to shoot him down right here and now. He's no better than Calton. But I figure we'd best take him along with us. We can't leave him here to go back and warn any of the others.'

'It's goin' to be dangerous draggin' a coyote like this with us, even if he doesn't have a gun,' said the old man thoughtfully. 'He'll wait for his chance to grab a gun and shoot us both in the back. I say we ought to put a bullet in him now. That way, at least, we'll be sure.'

'We'll take him with us,' Clint said flatly. 'He may come in useful as a shield if Calton does decide to fight.'

'Suit yourself,' muttered the other sharply. He eyed the man with distaste, clearly not trusting him. 'You goin' to watch him through the night?'

'I'll watch him,' Clint said, without emotion. He motioned the other forward and squatted down beside the fire, leaning his back against his saddle roll. He was still watchful for trickery on the other's part although he doubted if the man would try to make a break for it, not with a Winchester trained on him from a distance of a few feet and Clint had made it perfectly clear to him that he would shoot him without compunction the minute he tried to do anything funny.

Merriam curled himself up in his

blanket and was soon snoring loudly. Clint said harshly to the other. 'Reckon you'd better grab yourself some sleep. We got a hard day ahead of us tomorrow, catchin' up with that thievin' friend of yours.'

'You not goin' to tie me up?'

Clint gave a thin smile. 'I figure you might want to try to make a run for it durin' the night,' he said sardonically. He smiled steadily at the other across the fire.

The other gave a faint, mirthless grin and the implications of Clint's words were obviously not lost on him. Stretching himself out on the pine needles, the other closed his eyes and slept.

6

El Dorado

The moon went down and the dawn brightened slowly, a steely grey beginning to spread over the edge of the world. Beside the greying ashes of the fire, Merriam stirred in his blankets, then sat up, yawning, scratching his beard as he stared across at Clint. Then he got to his feet and began stirring up the fire, coaxing the last bit of redness from it, before throwing on more dried wood to start the blaze once more.

Placing the tin pan over the blaze, he cooked breakfast, handing some to their captive with an obvious reluctance. Clint guessed wryly that if the other had had his way he would have let the man go without anything to eat. That way, however, with hunger gnawing at the belly, a man was more ready to take risks and Clint wanted no trouble until they reached their destination.

'You get any sleep at all, Lanner?' taunted the outlaw harshly. There was a faint grin on his face and he lifted a long, low glance and laid it on Clint.

'Sure,' Clint nodded easily. 'If you hadn't been snorin' so loud, you'd have known.'

Whether the other believed that remark or not it was impossible to tell. But he relapsed into a sullen, savage-faced silence, ate his food slowly, washing it down with the hot coffee.

When the meal was finished, Clint said: 'I reckon you'd better pray that your mount stayed durin' the night. If not, you'll have a long and unpleasant ride on the mule.' He saw the red, angry blood rise to the other's face. They moved down to the trail and a few moments later, found the horse where it had wandered a little way to graze.

When they were saddled up and on the move, out into open country, Clint moved his mount up close behind the other's, keeping a watchful and wary eye on him. The other would be a fool to try anything without a gun and with a rifle at his back and now, he had the added incentive of throwing in his lot with them, at least until he came within shooting distance of his former partner who had double-crossed him. There were going to be fireworks once they did reach the El Dorado Mine, Clint reflected grimly.

The gunhawk wiped his forehead with the back of his sleeve, turned his head slowly. 'Can't we rest up for a while?' he asked.

'We'll rest up once we reach Broken Horse Pass,' said Clint, alert for any trickery on the other's part. 'In the meantime, just keep in the saddle and don't bat an eyelid.'

They came within sight of the pass a little before noon. The sun was blazing down from the zenith, the sky cloudless and the glaring, copper-coloured disc seemed to have burned all of the colour from the desert, the trackless wastes that lay in every direction, until there was only a bright white blankness that hurt the eyes and the shivering heat waves which shocked up at them from all sides.

'This is the place you spoke about, Clint,' said Merriam. He jerked a thumb in the direction of the high rocks that pinched down on two sides, with the narrow stony trail winding up until it passed between them. There was a harsh, glaring brightness here that sickened the mind and caused a throbbing ache at the back of the eyes.

'I can see why there ain't many people comin' out in this direction.' Clint scanned the area with a keen-eyed gaze, trying to memorize the details of the map in his mind and orientate himself with the pass as his central, focal point.

'You reckon you can find your way from here?' There was a note of anxiety in the prospector's tone. 'There ain't many other landmarks in the vicinity.'

'We head west from here,' Clint said

decisively. 'Should be a rock formation about a mile in that direction like an Indian's head.'

Merriam pursed his lips, making no reply. Then he swung his mount up towards the pass with the mule tagging along close behind.

Clint made to follow, then the outlaw said sharply: 'I thought you said we would rest up here for a while, Lanner.'

Clint nodded. 'All right.' He thrust the Winchester back into its scabbard, reined his mount and dropped nimbly from the saddle. He saw the man's hard eyes fasten on the guns at his belt, saw the instant cunning expression that flashed over his features and divined the other's thoughts.

'Better not try anythin' like that,' he said thinly. 'I don't particularly want to kill you right now, but if you make any move like that, I will. You've already told me everythin' I wanted to know, so you're no longer any use to us.'

The outlaw lapsed into a sullen silence, sat down with his legs doubled under him, scowling up at the sun. The breeze had died down completely now and the heat had increased, soaking through their shirts, bringing all of the moisture in their bodies boiling to the surface, sapping at their strength. Clint felt his eyes beginning to close, forced himself to remain alert with a conscious physical effort. Glancing about him through narrowed eyes, he sized up their situation. Certainly, Merriam had not exaggerated when he had said that this place was a regular hell-hole in the territory. They had spotted two water-holes on the way in and both had been dried out a long time before, so that the dust was now drifting in over the hard-baked, cracked earth.

From what little it had been possible to see of the country that lay beyond the pass, it was even worse there. Very little rain would fall in this area during the year and the blazing sun would suck what little there was out of the earth in a very short time. All the time they sat there in the terrible heat, he was aware of the outlaw's glance on him, cold and speculative. The other was only waiting his chance, he knew, and he would try to jump him before taking care of Merriam.

Ten minutes later, he hoisted himself heavily to his feet, wiped the sweat from his brow, then said harshly. 'All right, on your feet. We've wasted enough time here. Let's get started.'

For a moment, it looked as if the other intended to disregard Lanner. He drew his lips back savagely into a leering grin. 'You didn't get much sleep last night, did you, Lanner? Reckon you got little the night before too. Ain't no sense in denyin' it. I can see it in your eyes. You only got to relax once and — '

'You only got to make one false move and I'll blow a hole in the back of your head, mister.' Merriam spoke up from a couple of yards away, his hand hovering suggestingly close to the Sharps. 'Like Clint said, we got all we want from you. I'm all for shootin' you down right here, so don't make any mistake about whether I'll pull this trigger. That'd be the last mistake you make.'

Grunting under his breath, the other hauled himself upright, moved towards his horse and swung himself up into the saddle, face as black as thunder. It was clear that Merriam's words had struck home. They bored steadily onward through the yellow dust as the afternoon lengthened and the sun began its downward drift. Close on four o'clock, the land began to lift from its rolling flatness and off to their left, Clint spotted the cluster of rocks in the shape of an Indian's head. There was no mistaking it, even from that distance.

'Guess your memory is playing you straight, Clint,' muttered Merriam, nodding towards the rocks. 'How much further now?'

'Another five miles or so. We bear off to the north here.' He gestured to where the screen of hills crowded down on the edge of the plain. 'That should be it yonder.'

He felt rising excitement in him as he

spoke. Now they were close to the man who had robbed him that night on the trail. Turning his head a little, he shot a quick glance at their captive. He too, had a grudge against Calton. What would his reactions be when they finally caught up with the other?

Passing Indian's Head Rocks, they moved north. There were no trails here that one could follow. The mine was well hidden and it was plain to see why no one had found it since Everett. A legendary place of rich silver veins where a man could find enough of the precious metal to make himself rich. Small wonder men had fought and died for this knowledge.

Casting his glance ahead, he assessed the position, trying to put himself into Calton's shoes. The other would know that there was always the chance he might be followed, even here, that he would never give up following him. Perhaps now he was regretting that he had not killed him when he had had the chance.

The shadows cast by the rocks lengthened and their own shadows ran before them now as they moved deeper into the rugged, rocky country that lay ahead of them. Dust lifted under the feet of their horses as they moved forward with lowered heads. A wild, barren, tawny land in which they saw no sign of life beyond the occasional lizard that darted with a silent flash of colour among the rocks, and once they heard the vicious, warning rattle of a snake sunning itself in a smooth hollow on top of a rock. A land where death came swift and by several devious routes. Where a man who was unwary, was dead.

'Now comes the difficult part,' Clint said softly, licking his dry, cracked lips. 'There are so many wrong turnings one can take here.'

'These hills move back for close on fifty miles,' Merriam said hoarsely. 'And maybe a hundred miles long. If the mine is tucked away here it could take us an eternity to locate it.'

'It was marked clear enough on that map,' Clint intoned. He racked his brains as he reined his horse to a standstill, staring about him at the wild confusion of rocks and narrow clefts where a multitude of trails moved into the hills. In his mind's eye, he tried to recall all of the details on that scrap of tattered paper, the signs that had been written in that rambling scrawl and the directions given. So far, he had found all of the landmarks he recalled. But it only needed one slight mistake, one slip of the memory and they could become hopelessly lost in this wild country.

'I'll scout around and look for sign,' Merriam said. 'Could be we can pick up Calton's tracks and follow 'em in.'

'If we do, we'll have to keep a sharp look out. He can spot us miles away from up yonder in the hills and he'll fight to keep that mine.'

'Reckon you're right,' nodded the other; he scratched his beard. 'We'll be in the open most of the way in.'

Clint sat the saddle tensely while the

old-timer moved around, peering closely at the ground. Finally, he came after drawing a blank, shaking his head slowly. 'I figure he must've ridden up from some other direction if he ever got here,' he said thickly.

Clint glanced up at the sky to access how much more of the day there was still to run. He reckoned another three hours would see the sun well down to the horizon with night coming on, and here there was very little twilight. The change from daylight to the blackness of night was a swift thing. 'Let's get further into the hills,' he said shortly. 'Could be I'll be able to recognize some other landmark put on that map.'

Slowly, they wound their way into the tortuous hills. In places, the track they followed was so narrow that they were forced to move in single file and Clint kept close behind the outlaw, his hands near the guns at his belt. It would be at a time such as this, when their attention was directed at other things, that the other would choose his moment to make his play.

But for the time being, he still rode in moody silence, thinking his own thoughts. Maybe, Clint figured, he would wait until they located Calton. After all the man did not want to kill them, only to find himself utterly lost in these unfriendly hills with no way of getting back alive.

Just as the sun was dipping towards the peaks of the distant mountains, they rounded a sharply-angled bend in the trail, came out into a wide plateau, covered with a thin layer of drifting sand. The rocks lay in a rough circle on the perimeter of it, thrusting themselves up like teeth and halfway across it, Merriam suddenly reined in his mount and gave a sharp yell, leaning down from the saddle, pointing with his left hand.

Clint rode up. The tracks were clearly visible in the dust, partly wiped out here and there, where the breeze of the early morning had sent the sand over them.

'Single horseman,' said Merriam positively. He lifted himself in the saddle and threw a bright stare at the outlaw. 'Reckon this could be your friend. He's swung round to cut in from the east. Headed that way.' He pointed off to the north. 'I figure we can follow him easily enough now.'

'He doesn't know the hills. He'll have to stop pretty often to read that map and that's bound to slow him down,' Clint said tersely.

'All that silver which they say is in that mine is a strong enough incentive for a man to hurry. He won't be stoppin' long in any place until he does find it.'

'And you say there's no water to be had here?' Clint eyed Merriam shrewdly.

'That's it all right,' nodded the other. 'Ain't no streams run through this goddamned maze of hills. None that I've ever heard of anyway. If he took no water in with him, he's goin' to be mighty thirsty by the time we catch up with him and I've known men in that condition trade in all the silver they got for a canteen of warm water.'

'This man is a gambler of sorts,' Clint reminded the other. 'He'll take every chance in the book to keep both once he catches sight of us. It'll be dark soon and if he's spotted us by now, he may be gettin' ready to try to take us by surprise like this *hombre* did back at the camp.'

'Now hold up a minute, Lanner,' broke in the captive. 'I told you about last night. I figured it was Calton at that camp. He'd already double-crossed me with that map and I meant to get it back and find this place for myself. I didn't know it was you camped there. I'd figured you were still back in town.'

'Maybe you're tellin' the truth and maybe not,' Clint said tightly. 'I can't see that it makes much difference right now.'

'No? Listen, I want to see Calton dead as much as you do. And I can help you. I figure three guns against him would be better than two and a man you ain't sure of.'

'And the silver.' There was a note of sardonic amusement in Clint's voice.

'Split it three ways. You reckoned yourself there was plenty there for the three of us to be rich.'

Clint grinned mirthlessly. He shook his head slowly, saw the look of hope fade from the other's face to be replaced by the hard expression of cunning determination. 'You reckon we're just a couple of tinhorns. As soon as you had a gun you'd shoot both of us in the back and grab off all that silver for yourself.'

The rocks ahead of them lay deathly hushed in the fading sunlight as they pushed on over the level plateau, began to climb into the crests of the low ridges that ran on in a seemingly endless succession in front of them, hazed a little now by the approaching twilight, their hard contours softened slightly in the thrusting shadows that appeared among them. There was no timber here, only a few scattered patches of mesquite and prickly pear, plants which somehow managed to suck a little moisture from deep down inside this parched soil, growing and flourishing in spite of the cruel nature which had created this devil's cauldron, set off the beaten trail.

The land proved deceptive. Distances stretched themselves out and whereas they figured they could reach the taller ridges before nightfall it was soon apparent that they were further off than they appeared. They moved out of a narrow, steep-walled canyon and almost immediately found another in front of them. At one point, the rock arched over the canyon in a solid bow forming a natural tunnel, hollowed out of the solid rock by long ages of erosion. Pausing to glance about him, Clint saw that they had reached a tiny island of height here. Glancing back, he could make out the trail they had followed and in the distance, laying its black blob of shadow over the plain, were the

Indian's Head Rocks, standing out in loneliness against the bare stretch of the desert.

This was a cruel and vicious land, a place where men could die swiftly and easily. There had to be some places to make up for the lush greenness further to the north, he reflected idly, as he jogged along, eyes flicking from one side of the track to the other. In the lush wilderness where he had fought during the war, with every imaginable plant growing in profusion, nature had gone wild. Here, was the other extreme, a dry, waterless region, where the spectre of thirst lay over the land and the bitter-dry dust was a man's constant companion.

It seemed unlikely that this land would ever be tamed. It had that quality about it that spoke of an ability to defy anything that men might try to do. Now they rose with the short switchback courses, rode across a river of dust which seemed to be flowing down the side of the hills. Around them, daylight faded swiftly out of the sky and Clint, glancing up, noticed that the first bright stars were beginning to appear where the red flush of the sunset had long since faded from the western horizon and the night was already coming in.

Riding slowly and cautiously over ground that had been lifted and twisted into tumultuous shapes by some long-forgotten geological upheaval, they eventually reached a levelling off place. In the dim half-light, it was just possible to pick out the tracks in the dust where a single rider had headed that way not so long before. In his mind, Clint was certain now that it was Calton, the thief now somewhere in these hills. They were still on the upgrade of the hillside, pointed towards the high crests, even though the small plateau gave them some flatness, when they finally stopped to make camp.

On this particular night, Clint felt more tensed and nervous within himself than before. There was not only the outlaw to watch, but also the feeling of

Calton somewhere out there on the loose, potentially dangerous in spite of his deceptively mild and innocent appearance. At the moment, he wasn't sure how far they were from the El Dorado Mine, always assuming that it really existed and was not just a figment of someone's distorted imagination. That was a possibility that he continued to turn over in his mind after he had eaten cold. They did not dare build a fire here. They were out in the open, with no trees to provide them with a welcome screen and it was highly probable that Calton would spot a fire anywhere within a dozen miles of where he was.

Chewing unappetizingly on the cold slices of beef, washing it down with a little water from his canteen, had done little to ease the gnawing pangs of hunger in the pit of his stomach but at least it would help to keep him awake throughout the night.

'You figuring on staying awake all night again, Lanner?' asked the outlaw throatily. There was a note of faint amusement in his voice, coupled with a warning.

'Don't you go losin' sleep worryin' about me,' Clint told him forcefully. 'I'll get by without any sleep. Just you try to make a run for it on the strength of me not being awake to watch you and see how far you get.'

The man growled something deep in his throat, but it was impossible to make out any words and Clint sat back, leaning his shoulders against the tall rock behind him. He held the Winchester across his knees, levelled his gaze on the other until the man's gaze slipped away.

Somewhere in the night, new sounds lifted from the clinging silence. Clint listened to them as the silence deepened all about the plateau. He could see nothing, but faint murmurs of sound seemed to break and run on in little, idle fragments, presently dying.

Twice during the long night, the man lying in the blankets a few feet away, made a move as if to crawl away, only to halt in his tracks as the muzzle of the rifle swung on him, covering his body. The moon rose, flooded everything with its cold light, shadowed the rocks about them so that it was easy to imagine shapes moving among them. He felt chill as the coldness of the air, flowed down the hillside, but his face was hot and sticky and when he took off his hat, sweat dripped down his forehead and he tasted salt on his lips. There was a continuing ache in his chest and he would have liked to sleep, but he could not trust the old man to watch their prisoner. Not that he doubted the other's capability to shoot if there was any trouble, but it was possible that he could be tricked into losing control of his rifle.

The moon traced its yellow trail across the arch of the heavens and then it was cold, grey dawn. He stretched himself, got to his feet and moved to the edge of the plateau, keeping an intermittent watch on the man lying in the middle of the clearing. Climbing on to the narrow ledge, he stared off into the hills that lay to the north.

Several thoughts chased themselves around in his mind. Was the fabulous El Dorado Mine somewhere in there? Had Calton discovered it using the map he had stolen? If he had, was he still alive, or was he lying there dying, or dead, from thirst, having overlooked the simple precaution of taking water with him in his greed for silver?

He remained there for several minutes while the dawn brightened and details resolved themselves all about him. The tracks they had discovered the previous evening continued to head towards the north. It was evident that Calton — for he was certain now that his was the identity of the rider who preceded them — had continued on into the wild country still ahead of them. He had been hurrying, that much was clear from a cursory examination of the tracks, pushing his horse to its limit. That clearly meant he considered himself on safe ground, that he had been thinking of nothing at the time but of getting to the mine as quickly as possible. It was the action of a man whose thoughts were fastened on only one thing, a man controlled and motivated by greed. Such a man would turn and fight like a rat in a trap if he was cornered.

What jerked his mind back to the present was a slight movement far off in the rocks to one side. He swung his head to stare straight in the direction where he had noticed it, but could see nothing. The shadows there were still tricky, and he knew it could have been nothing more than a trick of his tired mind. But he continued to watch, his whole body tensed and poised.

A shadow moved, slipped from one boulder to another. He had seen the man for only a brief second when he had darted across that open space between the boulders, but what he had seen was enough for him to have made a positive identification. It had been

Calton. There had been no mistaking that flowing black frock-coat, the small build of the other. Crouching down, he watched the other's approach, judging that it would take the best part of half an hour before he reached the edge of the plateau. He slithered back from his perch, knew that the other had not spotted him.

'Seen something?' queried the man in the blankets. He propped himself up on one elbow, eyeing Clint sneeringly. 'You look like you just seen a ghost.'

'Not a ghost exactly,' Clint retorted sharply. 'Just your pal Calton headin' this way. Reckon he figures he'd better check on things every so often just in case anybody is on his tail.'

'Calton!' The other hissed the name through clenched teeth. He struggled to his feet. 'Where is he?'

'Don't start gettin' any fast ideas,' Clint warned him harshly. 'We'll take care of Calton. First I want to have a little talk with him, find out whether he still has that map on him and if not, where he's hidden it. If he has put it somewhere I want to know before he's dead.'

'Don't you reckon I got the same kind of score to settle with this double-crosser as you have?'

'Could be that you see it that way,' Clint murmured slowly, but there was a hard gleam in his eye. 'Unfortunately, I don't. You'll stay back and keep well out of this or I'll drill you.'

The other's features set in a sullen expression and his glance fell for a second to the guns at Clint's belt. Then he gave a quick shrug, turned away. 'If you feel that way, then go ahead,' he said thinly. 'Only I reckon I'd better warn you, he's an excellent shot even though he does prefer that Derringer of his.'

'Thanks for the warnin'.' Clint motioned towards the far edge of the plateau. 'Now you get back over there and stay out of this.'

The other stretched himself slowly. 'Suit yourself.' He started to move away, then bent. 'Mind if I take my blankets with me? I dislike lying on the bare rocks.'

'All right. But make it quick.'

The other grabbed the corner of his blankets and it was in that moment, as Clint flicked a quick glance towards Merriam, already getting to his feet, that the other acted, jerking the blankets up and straight for Clint's face. Sand had drifted on to them during the night and it stung at Clint's eyes. Instinctively, unable to help himself, he staggered back, blinking rapidly several times, shaking his head as savage lances of pain jarred through his eyes and forehead, blinding him. The irritating grains seared his vision, bringing tears that blurred his eyesight.

With a wild, harsh oath, the other hurled himself forward, one huge, beefy fist lashing at Clint's jaw. Acting more by instinct than anything else, Clint side-stepped, covered up with his arms and elbows, turning his head swiftly to one side so that the blow, which would have knocked him cold had it landed flush on its target, merely grazed his chin in passing, knuckles scraping the skin. But there had been all of the other's weight behind that blow, and although only a glancing impact, it was sufficient to knock him backward, his shoulders slamming hard against the rock behind him. Clint seemed to be seeing things through a shimmering curtain of red, the other's features blurring and wavering in front of him. He lashed out savagely and more by luck than judgement, caught the other on the side of the head as he rushed in. The outlaw staggered, fell back under the blow, emitting a curious bleat of agony through his clenched teeth. Then he came in again, determined not to let this chance of escape slip through his fingers. Over the man's shoulder, Clint saw Merriam hopping around from one foot to the other, the Sharps in his hands, unable to fire for fear of hitting him.

Hard fists hammered a tattoo on Clint's chest, bruising his ribs and threatening to drive all of the air from his body. He struggled to retain a hold on his consciousness. There was a hard edge of rock grinding into his back between the shoulder blades and he gritted his teeth hard as pain seared through his body. Quick to seize his advantage the other threw his arms around Clint's body, forcing him back, leaning all of his weight on him, tightening his grip by linking his fingers together in the small of his back and thrusting his chin into Clint's chest, pressing down with all of his strength. Clint felt his spine begin to bend, knew that he had to get out of this punishing, killing grip soon or his back would be broken by the other. The human spine could take only so much punishment before it snapped like a rotten twig.

Through the haze of pain in front of his stultified vision, he saw the man's grinning features, lips twisted back in a sneering grin of triumph, he felt the other's breath on his face. His eyeballs still stung terribly from the itching grains that had been thrown into them and he longed to be able to rub them in an attempt to ease the pain.

There was only one way to get out of this bear hug. Letting all of the air whoosh from his lungs, he allowed his body to go completely limp. The other instinctively relaxed his grip, confident that Clint was finished and in that same moment, as he was off balance, Clint jerked his arms from his sides with all of his remaining strength. Taken completely by surprise, the other fell back, arms flailing. There was no time for Clint to draw his guns, the other was still too close and it would be difficult to be sure of killing him outright. Not only that, but it needed only one gunshot to warn Calton where they were and as this outlaw had so rightly said, Calton was a dangerous killer.

For a long moment, he found it difficult to move. His back felt as though it had been stretched on the rack and there was a painful ache in every limb and muscle. He sobbed air down into his tortured lungs, waited a moment for his vision to clear and in that time, the outlaw came on balance again, was moving towards him with the killing fever visible in his eyes, tight fists moved by his sides. He was determined not to make the same mistake of underestimating Clint again. Mouth working, he came forward, feinted to his right, then swung up with a sharp, jabbing left. Clint rode the blow, sucked another gulp of air down into his lungs, then lashed savagely at the grinning face in front of him, felt a little sense of satisfaction as his knuckles connected with a solid jolt on the other's mouth. The gunhawk took the blow with a savage bellow of animal rage, stood his ground, and then continued to come in, throwing all caution to the winds in his anger. His one object seemed to be to strangle Clint and get his hands on the guns still in their holsters. He rightly ignored Merriam, knowing that the other represented little danger to him, would not dare to fire the rifle he still held.

Another flurry of blows sent Clint reeling. The other did not seem to be troubled over much by the blows he himself was hammering home. It was as if the man were made of granite for all the effect they were having. Yet they must surely be slowing him down somewhat. With an effort, he gathered himself, threw two short piston-like blows into the bobbing weaving face, felt both strike on the other's cheek, knuckles grazing the flesh over the high cheek-bones. The man's knees buckled, but still he found the strength to remain upright and slug it out, gasping harshly for breath, his face flushed now with the exertion and the hammering it had received. Two more blows from the rock-like fists hit Clint on the side of the skull as the man drove forward. Clint shifted his body, knowing what the man intended to do next. It was the only chance the other had of winning this fight and he seemed to realize it. His knee came up hard, but already Clint was twisting away and the hard blow merely took him on the side of the thigh, throwing him off balance a little but doing no more damage.

Gritting his teeth tightly, he cocked his fist, saw the other stumble forward as the impetus of the last move swung him on to his toes. As the man's head went forward, Clint swung down with the side of his straightened hand, caught the other on the back of the neck. A thinner neck would have cracked under that blow; as it was the man emitted a faint coughing gasp and slumped on to his knees, almost out on his feet.

Clint stood away from him, ready for any further trouble, but the man was swaying forward, barely conscious. Grabbing him by the front of his shirt, Clint hauled him on to his feet, thrust his face close to the other's and hissed. 'I warned you what would happen if you tried anything like that.' His voice was husky and edged with tension in spite of the grip he had on himself. 'Seems to me you have to be taught a real lesson before it sinks into that thick skull of yours.' He thrust the man away from him. For a moment the other swayed, his eyes blank, mouth open and working spasmodically, lips moving but no sound coming out. Then he toppled on to his back and lay there, chest heaving, the muscles of his throat corded and constricted as he tried to suck air into his chest and seemed to be totally unable to do so.

There would be no more trouble from him, Clint reflected as he moved away, glancing up to where Merriam had moved in close, still gripping the rifle, his face full of concern. He stood looking down at the body of the outlaw on the rock, then he said hoarsely: 'Seems to me he asked for that, Clint. Now maybe you'll see why I told you to shoot the critter before he made any trouble for us. Perhaps next time, you'll listen to an old-timer like me.'

'I figure the next time is nearly on us,' Clint said a little breathlessly. He inclined his head in the direction of the rocky ledge than ran around the perimeter of the plateau to the north. 'Calton's out there. I spotted him a few moments ago. That was why this *hombre* made his try then. Either he was hopin' to warn his former partner, or he wanted to make sure we were out of the way and he'd take care of him by himself, grabbing off everything.'

'Calton yonder,' Merriam nodded his head, eased himself forward, keeping himself low. 'What are we waitin' fer?'

'Keep your head down, old-timer,' Clint said warningly. 'He's a crack shot with that Derringer of his.'

Cautiously, Merriam lifted his head above the level of the rocks directly in front of him. He turned his head slowly, the whiskers jutting out from his features.

'Don't see a goshdarned thing,' he

murmured. 'You sure you spotted him, Clint?'

'He's there all right, make no mistake about that. Whether he knows we're here is a different matter. I'm pretty certain he didn't spot me, but he may have heard something. Sound travels well in a place like this and if he picked up the sounds of that fight, he'll have scurried back under cover and we won't see anything of him until he opens fire.'

'Cunning little customer,' grunted the other. He lowered himself back on to the smooth, dusty ground of the plateau, then wriggled away to the left, still clutching the faithful Sharps in his right hand. Clint threw a quick glance over his shoulder at the man who lay on the other side of the plateau. The outlaw was still out cold, lying face-down on the dust, legs stretched out straight behind him. That chopping blow on the back of the neck ought to keep him out of this for some time yet, Clint reflected. Whatever happened, he didn't want the other to come round just when they had Carton pinned down. There was no telling what trouble the other could cause them, catching them from the rear.

He jerked his head up sharply as a sudden gunshot barked from the pale-lit rocks. At first, he thought it was Merriam firing at shadows, then he spotted the other, crouched well down behind a clump of loosely-tumbled boulders and the screeching howl of the ricochet still hung in the air where the bullet had struck the top of one of the boulders and whined off into the distance. So Calton knew where they were and there had been nothing wrong with the man's aim either.

Cautiously, he wormed his way around one of the boulders in front of him, squinted up against the growing light of the dawn, eyes slitted, attempting to pick out the little gambler. He could make out nothing. Wherever the other was, he was undeniably keeping himself well hidden, knowing perhaps that there were two men against him now and he would need all of his subtlety to keep out of trouble and turn events in his favour.

Clint's face was hard and set in grim lines of determination. Every nerve and instinct screamed incessantly at him to get to his feet, draw the other's fire in the hope of pinpointing his position. But he fought down the feeling. He had been taken in by the mild-mannered little man before and he did not want to risk it a second time. Strategy was essential here. Waving Merriam to move around in a circle, he edged forward into the tall rocks. His boots made only the barest whisper of sound on the stone as he slid forward into the greyness. Another shot broke the clinging stillness, this time it had been Merriam who had fired. He recognized the sharp bark of the rifle, eased his head around the edge of rock, expecting Calton to make some move now that the old prospector had given his position away.

But Calton was being equally cunning, determined not to be drawn in this way. There was no return fire from the rocks. Gingerly, Clint moved forward, every nerve in him stretched almost to breaking point. In a small gully that led up through the rocks, Clint paused to debate the position. If he continued forward like this, there was a a good chance he might move right past Calton without seeing him. If he stayed here, then Calton might be edging forward in Merriam's direction, hoping to take the other by surprise. It was one of those quick decisions, ended immediately. He wriggled along the narrow wrinkle in the rocks, reached the top and looked intently about him. From here, one of the highest points in this maze of rocks, he was able to look down on the rest of the area. Almost at once, he spotted Calton, lying face down in a narrow cleft, where two boulders lifted precipitously on either side. From there, the other could watch almost every direction of approach and pick off anyone moving towards him. Clint was above and slightly behind the gambler, his black coat standing out clearly now, where the shadows were dark patches of midnight.

Lifting his gaze a little, he saw Merriam. The prospector was perhaps two hundred yards from the spot where Calton lay, and it was obvious that the gambler had already seen the other, was merely biding his time, waiting for him to move out into an open patch of ground before drilling him. Merriam would be dead before he knew that he had been seen, that his presence there had even been suspected.

Gently, Clint eased the Winchester forward, gave it a quick glance to ensure it was loaded, then eased off the safety catch. Calton did not suspect that he was there, considered himself to be perfectly safe. He probably figured that Clint was still back in the plateau, keeping an eye on the outlaw. He saw the gambler lift the tiny, innocent-looking Derringer, was even able to see the expression of anticipation on the man's face. The other was enjoying this, this waiting for the right moment to strike.

Clint felt a coldness in his face, a tightness that grew swiftly in his chest. His body still ached from the bruising it had received, but he was able to ignore this now. His enemy lay in front of him, but he wanted the other to know who was killing him and why. He did not intend to shoot Calton in the back. The gambler was going to know who pulled the trigger that sent him hurtling into eternity.

Sucking in a heavy gust of wind, he let it come out slowly through his nostrils. He lay rigid for several seconds, watching Merriam's painfully slow approach, judging the moment when the other would reach that open stretch of ground and get ready to move across it. Merriam was wary. He had recognized this danger even before he had reached it, clearly did not relish the idea of moving over that open patch, but clearly recognizing that there was no other choice left open to him but to go back the way he had come and waste several precious minutes.

The old man had reached the end of the narrow gully which had afforded him protection for almost twenty yards. Now he was poised on the edge of the open ground, contemplating the situation, turning over the danger in his mind, trying to decide on the best course to take. Clint gauged the moment nicely. He saw the prospector gather his legs under him, ready for that quick, brief dash which would carry him into the cover of the rocks on the other side, but which, unknown to him, would carry him forward to death. A quick bullet would be waiting for him the moment he moved out of cover of the gully.

He saw Calton tensed, lift the Derringer, holding it easily in his hand, taking a careful aim as he waited, finger on the trigger. Standing up among the rocks, Clint said loudly.

'Drop that gun, Calton.'

He saw the other stiffen, but he still kept a tight-fisted hold on the gun.

More harshly and loudly this time: 'I said drop that gun, or I'll let you have it in the back.'

A pause, then Calton said tightly. 'That you standing behind me, Lanner?'

'You guessed right. You didn't think you could steal my map and still get away with it, did you?'

He saw the almost imperceptible sag of the other's shoulders as a wave of defeat seemed to sweep over him, but he was not fooled as the man lowered his hand and half turned. Quick as a flash, Calton whirled, moving with an agility that belied his age. The Derringer in his hand swung up to where Clint stood. It was evident that he had been judging exactly where Clint had been standing, by listening to his voice. In a blur of speed, Clint's hands lifted the heavy rifle, his finger squeezed gently on the trigger. Both gunshots seemed to blast at the same moment, throwing loud, reverberating echoes back from the rocks that ringed them round. Clint heard the faint whisper of the slug going past his head, cutting so close that he felt the scorching touch of it against his cheek. Then he saw Calton standing in the small hollow, his arm lowering, the Derringer pointing at the rocks near his feet. His eyes were turned towards Clint with an almost bemused expression as though unable to believe what had happened. For a moment, they retained their brightness. Then the death glaze spread swiftly over them, something red gushed from his mouth and he toppled forward into the dust, head striking the rocks with a sickening thud. Slowly, Clint moved down, picking his way carefully among the boulders and knife-edged stones that littered the place. Merriam came up the narrow wrinkle in the rocks, lowering his arm to his side. He stared down at the dead gambler with no show of emotion on his face.

'He was just gettin' ready to drop you the minute you moved out into the open,' Clint said tonelessly. 'I had him spotted from up yonder, but I wanted him to know who had killed him.' He went down on one knee as he spoke, turned the dead man over and went carefully through his pockets. In one of them, he found the map and the silver nugget.

Merriam said: 'That the piece of paper you've been lookin' for?'

Clint nodded. 'Not much for so many men to be killed over, is it?' He smoothed it out on the rock, examined it closely.

'You reckon he found the place and then back-tracked along the trail, lookin' for us?' queried the older man.

'Could be,' Clint said a mite impatiently. He pointed with his finger at the map. 'Here's Indian's Head Rocks and this is the trail we took. He must've come from this direction and this cross marks the position of the mine itself. My guess is he found it and then reckoned he might have been followed and came back just to make sure.'

Merriam glanced down at the body in front of him. 'Reckon he won't be gettin' any of that silver now,' he said tautly. He glanced up at the brightening heavens. It was already growing red in the east where the sun would soon come up over the distant rim of the world like a vast explosion of fire and flame somewhere just out of sight in the other regions. 'It's goin' to be another hot day. I figure we'd better make tracks.'

Clint nodded, folded the map and placed it carefully in his pocket, Leaving the body of the gambler where he had fallen, they made their way back to the wide plateau. The horses and the burro stood patiently where they had been tethered the previous night. Then Clint let his gaze move around the rock-strewn flatness and a curse came from between his lips. There was no sign of the outlaw he had knocked out only a little while before. The other must have come to and taken his chance of slipping away into the rocks.

His face was tight and almost murderous as he looked sharply at Merriam. His face was hard-bitter as he said: 'That critter must've had a thicker neck than I figured. He could be anywhere by now. Probably headin' back to town and — '

'That ain't likely,' muttered the old prospector. He nodded in the direction of the horses. 'He left his mount behind. Nobody gettin' ready to hit the trail out of here would do that. He's hidin' somewhere in the rocks, bidin' his time, waitin' for a chance to jump us.'

Clint pondered that for a long moment, letting his keen-eyed gaze wander among the rocks and tumbled boulders. He could see no sign of the other, but what the oldster had said was evidently true. The outlaw was as determined to get his hands on that silver as they were, knew by now that his erstwhile companion was dead and the map was back in Clint's hands. He would be unable to do anything about attacking them since he was unarmed, but so long as he remained out of sight he would be able to wait until he had an opportunity to take them by surprise.

'Maybe we should've killed him when we had the chance,' Clint muttered under his breath.

'You still goin' to follow that map, even though he's out there somewhere, watchin' every move we make?'

'Reckon we got no other choice,' Clint moved towards the horses. 'Better take these critters with us even though it's goin' to be difficult along that trail. If we don't he may try to head back here once he finds out where the mine is, and leave us stranded.'

* * *

Cuffing his hat on to the back of his sweat-marked hair, Clint sat in the saddle, resting his hands squarely on the saddle-horn as he tilted his head back and looked up into the towering rocks which rose sheer and high on either side of the long, narrow canyon. His face was powdered with the dust that had lifted around them all morning, getting into the folds of his skin, forming long itching lines of raw flesh along his cheeks and neck. Merriam came up alongside him, reined his mount, then hooked one leg over the saddlehorn and twisted up a cigarette, proffering the tobacco pouch to the other. Clint considered it for a moment, then shook his head. His mouth felt dry and parched, his lips cracked and he knew the smoke would only make it worse. They had only half a canteen of water apiece and during the whole of the long climb through this nightmare wilderness, they had seen no sign of water. Merriam was convinced there was none to be had in this wild territory and now Clint was beginning to believe him. There was one river flowing out across the plains to the north of this range of high hills, and he had reckoned to himself that it must have had its source somewhere here, but now, as time went on and the dry bitter scent of dust was their only companion in the heat-filled silence, he was growing more and more certain that if the stream which eventually formed that river did have its origins here, it must be many miles from where they were. He glanced down at the map for what seemed the hundredth time since they had set out that morning. If they had been following the directions right, the mine should be somewhere just beyond this narrow-cut canyon.

'Not goin' to be easy getting through there,' Merriam opined. He lit the cigarette, blew smoke into the still air, his wrinkled face twisted into a faint scowl.

'It's good cover for a dry-gulcher, if that *hombre* did manage to get ahead of us,' Clint observed. He let his gaze lift to the narrow ledges, just visible above the winding trail through the canyon. Thoughtfully, he ran his eye along them.

'You figure he might be somewhere up there, ready to drop one of them rocks down on top of us?'

'Could be — and I don't want to underestimate that coyote. I've done that once too often. We know he's somewhere close by. We didn't make very fast progress through those hills, probably slower than he could have done on foot. Easing the horses along those tracks must've slowed up our travel. He could have swung around us without being seen.'

Merriam nodded his head slowly, drew deeply on the cigarette. He screwed up his lips slightly. Brow furrowed, he said grimly: 'One thing been worryin' me since we've been ridin'.'

'What's that?' Clint glanced sideways at the other.

'We've been figurin' all along that he ain't armed. Supposin' he is. He could shoot us down the minute we move into that canyon.'

'Now where in hell could he get a gun out here?' Clint snapped tautly.

Slowly, deliberately, the other went on: 'We forgot about that gun that Calton had. Only a Derringer, but it could be lethal and he may have circled around and picked it up before settin' out on our tail.'

Clint's mouth tightened. It was a thought that had never occurred to him. Once more, he felt the cold seething anger flood through him, but this time it was directed against himself. It was something he should never have overlooked. Of course the gunman would check on Calton's body for a gun on the chance that they had been stupid enough to leave that small, but deadly, Derringer. And now they had given him the means of defeating them.

'Then he could well be up there right now,' he said through thinned lips. 'We'd better ride real slow and careful now.'

They both set their mounts moving again, heading them forward into the knife-edged canyon, hoofs ringing like metal on metal as they rode on to the smooth rock of the canyon floor. Clint rode especially alert, tensely, his rifle across his knees, eyes raking every inch of the trail on either side of them, ahead and above. But the rocks that studded the narrow ledges overlooking the trail here were so numerous and thickly clustered that he knew deep down that the chances of spotting any dry-gulcher's position before that small Derringer spat death down at them, were pretty remote.

It was noon now and here and there they were forced to dismount and lead the horses forward where rocks littered the canyon floor. Down here they were in deep shadow. It was doubtful if the sunlight ever reached the canyon floor even at high noon. The chances were that they were riding into a trap, that the outlaw had circled around them and climbed the slope so that he would be able to see some way out into the badlands.

The going was tough now, really tough. Although there was no sunlight down in the canyon, it acted as a heat trap, soaking up the heat from the higher slopes and reflecting it downward. Every breath Clint drew into his lungs hurt like fire and it was as if thousands of red-hot needles were being thrust into his flesh. He rubbed his eyes, knew that this was only making things worse, the dust abrading his eyeballs until his vision blurred even worse than before.

Gradually, the crowding walls of the canyon moved away from the trail and it widened out appreciably. The tricky overtones of shadow and dust endowed each boulder with human form and he felt the little itch between his shoulder blades growing stronger with every step his horse took that led them deeper into the rocks. As he rode, he was aware mostly of his tiredness and the physical discomfort which came from long days in the saddle.

Then, almost without warning, the canyon opened and they rode out into sunlight and open country. The rocky walls fell away behind them and Clint let his breath gush from his nostrils in a sigh of relief. Every indication was that the outlaw was still behind them. He would not have overlooked a position such as that for an ambush if he had managed to get ahead of them to lay a gun trap.

'There,' said Merriam suddenly. He stood in his saddle, feet braced in the stirrups, pointing with one hand.

Clint narrowed his eyes against the sudden glare of sunlight, saw the wooden shack that had been built close to a sheer wall of rock less than three hundred yards away. Low-roofed, it was a typical prospector's shack set close to mine workings which could just be seen in the cliff wall.

'That's it,' Merriam yelled. His face was alight with excitement. 'The lost El

Dorado Mine. Y'know, I always figured it was some sort of legend, that it never really existed. But there it is.'

He touched spurs to his mount, rode forward at a swift gallop. In spite of the vague apprehension in his mind, Clint followed him. Reining their mounts in front of the shack, they slid from the saddles, dust lifting about them. Clint kicked open the door and went inside. Slowly, his eyes accustomed themselves to the gloom there. Dust lay everywhere and at first sight it looked as if the place had lain deserted for years. Then he noticed the marks in the dust on the floor, knew that Calton had reached this place. But if that were so, then where was the gambler's horse? He had been on foot when they had spotted him back there near the plateau, and they had seen no sign of it along the trail.

'Some food here,' Merriam said. 'No sign of any water. You reckon Calton might have been headin' back in search of water when he stumbled across us?'

'Might have been,' Clint agreed. 'Funny he didn't take his horse with him.'

'Say, that's right,' nodded the other. 'Wonder where he could've left it?'

'Inside the mine workings, maybe. That way, it would be out of sight if anyone did manage to follow him this far and take a look around the place.'

A quick search of the shack revealed little. There were signs that someone had prepared a quick meal some time earlier and the remains of it were still on the small table.

'Let's take a look inside the mine, see what we've really got here, whether it was worth all this trouble.' Clint moved to the door. Outside, he paused to throw a quick glance around the rocky clearing. A deep stillness lay over everything and in the distance, the canyon brooded in the sunlight, the bright glare glancing off the topmost rocks in an almost eye-searing light. The canyon, he noticed now, guarded the only possible route into the clearing and the mine workings. The other directions of approach led through some of the roughest and most treacherous country he had seen. Like Merriam had said some time before, a man could hold off an army here if he had enough food and water and ammunition to last out.

There was no sign that the outlaw had caught up with them. Maybe they were being too cautious about him. It was possible that he was making far slower progress than they and was still a mile or more behind them, struggling along that rocky trail with the glaring sun of early afternoon flooding down on him, making things even worse.

Leaving their horses outside the shack, they made their way on foot to the entrance of the mine workings. A mass of small boulders lay just outside the entrance and a quick glance was enough to tell Clint that someone had used dynamite here to widen the opening. Hidden away in the fastnesses of these tall hills, set so far from the beaten trail, there was little wonder that the whereabouts of this fabulous, almost legendary, mine had been lost. Clint stood for a long second outside the gaping hole in the side of the living mountain, trying to peer into the gloom. He felt a moment's apprehension as he stood there. He was a man born to the saddle and the wide, open spaces of the mountains and the vast prairies, and he did not like the idea of being underground, with all of that blackness about him and the terrible, crushing weight of those millions of tons of rock above his head. But he swallowed his fear with an effort, and followed Merriam inside. The other seemed perfectly at his ease as he moved into the cold, gloomy interior.

Merriam explained, as they stood perhaps twenty yards inside the opening, that the tunnel which had been drilled into the rock probably extended for several hundred yards and might be interlaced by other, smaller tunnels running off to either side, forming a regular honeycomb of passages there inside the mountain.

Clint listened to the other with only part of his mind. From what he was able to see, it was clear that a lot of work and effort had gone into opening up this mine, searching out the rich seams of ore, the veins which contained the precious silver. Somehow, possibly because of the war, it had been abandoned, or there had been other workings opened up and men had drifted away to mine these.

Not until some years later, when Everett and that other prospector had stumbled on the mine once more and realized that here was a real bonanza, had the legend of the El Dorado Mine been reborn and men had been killed in an attempt to get that map which gave a clue as to its whereabouts. And now, he and Merriam were actually standing inside it. He watched the other move over to the rough rock and run his fingers over it, exploring the cracks and crevices there, feeling for deep fissures.

Merriam struck a match, peered closely at the rock as Clint went forward and peered over his shoulder.

'Find anythin'?' Clint asked.

'Could be. This part of the mine has probably already been worked out. Not much here.' Turning, he began to work his way deeper into the shaft, picking his way carefully over the upthrusting boulders that lay under their feet. Now, it was almost pitch black here with only a faint light filtering in to them from the opening in the distance. There had been metal rails here once, Clint noticed, but they had been torn up from the rocky floor and taken away, maybe to one of the other mines in the vicinity. Stumbling a little, he followed close on the other's heels, straining his eyes to see in the darkness. There was the feeling of claustrophobia in his mind, tightening its grip on him, in spite of all he could do to force it down. The walls shut them in and his hands were torn by the sharp-edged rocks.

Merriam paused again, struck another match and peered forward in the faint orange flare. 'This is where Everett must've started work,' he called over his shoulder, his words booming back at them from the rocks.

In the pale light of the match, Clint was able to make out the narrower tunnel that dipped away from the main shaft, striking almost at right angles into the rock. Unlike the main tunnel, here the walls were rough-hewn. Everett had either not dared to use dynamite here to blast away the rock, or he had not had any to use. Whatever the reason, he had hacked away at the hard rock with a pick, working his way slowly forward.

'This must be where he made his rich strike,' Merriam said, lowering his voice. 'From what little I recall about the El Dorado Mine, it was supposed to have been worked out a couple of years before the war started. Here, they were well away from the main area of fighting, but some other mines were started when more strikes were made along the trail down towards New Mexico. I reckon most of the miners moved south and it wasn't until Everett came along and started prospectin' again, that he found this rich seam here.'

'Think you can locate it again?'

'I reckon so.' The other nodded, edged forward once more, picking his way over the rocks underfoot. Clint followed close behind, trailing one hand on the wall of the tunnel. Here and there, his fingers encountered a patch of slimy moisture on the rock, where a thin trickle of water came down from the roof of the tunnel. The find heartened him a little. It was possible that here, under the rocks, they might find a small stream to replenish their meagre water supplies. The thought of all those long, weary miles they had to cover before they reached the river, made him realize that even if they did succeed in finding this rich seam of silver, water was the prime requirement.

Merriam said over his shoulder: 'Better keep your head down, Clint. The room here is pretty cramped and the roof comes down.'

Gingerly, Clint reached up with his hand, felt the undersurface of the roof easily less than a foot above his head and a few moments later, it came even lower.

Three minutes later, they were forced to crawl. Occasionally, Merriam lit a match and examined the roughhewn, rocky walls around them, peering closely at them. Finally, he gave a sharp exhalation of satisfaction, pulled a small knife from his jacket and prised something loose from the rock, handing it back to Clint before the flickering light of the match died.

In the brief glare, Clint was able to see that it was a big nugget of silver almost the same as that which he had found together with the map in Everett's boot.

'That's it,' he said harshly. 'Then this

must be the place that Everett found.'

'Don't reckon there's much doubt about it.' The other's voice drifted back to him. 'But we'll need to get more light down here. There should be a lamp back in the shack. Once we get that, we'll be able to dig out some of this silver.'

★ ★ ★

The sun had dropped appreciably by the time they came out of the mine and stepped into the clearing. Already, most of the land here was in deep shadow as the tall hills cut off the light of the sun, now dipping to the west. There was still plenty of warmth in the air, a warmth that would last until shortly after sundown, when the dark would come bringing the bitter cold of night in the hills.

'I figure we'd better wait until the morning before goin' back in there,' said Merriam, hunting around on the shelves at the back of the shack for the food which lay there. He rummaged around for a while, then said in disgust: 'I reckon we can't eat any of this. I'd better bring in some of the supplies from the saddle-bags and make us a meal.'

When he came back, he brought in some of the wood from the side of the shack and soon had a fire going. Minutes later, there was the fragrance of frying bacon inside the shack and Clint sat close to the door, although not in line with it, allowing himself to relax a little. He had been so long on the alert that he felt dissatisfied now and Merriam looked up curiously at him from the fire.

'Nobody will come this way unless that *hombre* manages to catch up with us, and from here we'll be able to see him some way off. He won't be able to take us by surprise and that Derringer he's carrying won't be of any use to him at that distance.' He gave a brief nod in the direction of the canyon. 'He's got to come that way, no other way to get into this clearing.'

With an effort, Clint forced himself to relax. The other was right, of course. The outlaw had to come in through the canyon, the latter course seemed more doubtful. There would be no advantage to the other to take that roundabout route and waste both time and strength climbing those sharply-rising trails. The fire had caught a firm hold now and added its heat to the small cabin.

'Better get some grub into your belly,' said Merriam, a few moments later as Clint continued to sit there, watching the canyon. 'You'll feel better and after that, you can have some sleep. I'll keep watch from here.'

'You sure?' Clint took the plate the other held out to him, began to eat ravenously.

'What d'you mean, am I sure? Don't you trust me to stay awake and keep my eyes open?' There was indignation in the other's gruff tones. He nodded towards the Sharps rifle leaning in the corner of the shack. 'I was handling one of those guns before you were born.'

'Sure, sure,' Clint nodded his head quickly at the other's outburst. 'I reckon you're right. I do need some sleep.' He told himself that there was little chance of the old prospector being jumped and there were still several hours of daylight left during which he could snatch a little sleep.

Finishing his meal, he smoked a cigarette, standing in the doorway of the cabin, taking stock of the scene outside. The whole clearing was, he noticed, completely boxed in, with deep, precipitous sides except where the canyon led into it. He felt reasonably confident that there was no other way in and the doorway of the shack faced directly in the direction of the canyon mouth.

Grinding the butt of the cigarette under his heel, he moved back into the cabin, lowered himself on to the bunk against the rear wall. The long days and nights on the trail, lacking proper sleep because of the necessity of watching that outlaw they had picked up, had already begun to catch up on him. Even the hard, lumpiness of the straw-filled tick of the bunk made little difference to the weariness in his body. He closed his eyes and thought for a moment of the man on the trail, crouched somewhere among the rocks perhaps, watching the narrow canyon and maybe wondering if they were waiting for him, laying a gun trap along its narrow length, knowing that he was following them. The thought troubled him and he thought: *He's got to catch up on us now that he has no horse. Otherwise there can be no going back for him and without water, he'll be dead in a couple of days.* The longer the other delayed, the more dangerous would his position become and the more dangerous he would be.

He heard Merriam rise and then seat himself close to the door. There was the faintly metallic clatter of the rifle as the barrel struck against the wall. He meant to rise and tell the other that he did not need any sleep at all, that he would keep watch with him, but he thought inwardly, I'll get up in a minute, and meantime I'll just lie here and rest for a while.

When he opened his eyes again, it was nearly dark. He could just make out the shape of the other seated near the door, the rifle across his knees. The man looked round as he stirred, got to his feet.

'You slept hard,' he said. 'Guess you needed that.'

Clint swung his legs to the floor, stood up. 'Any trouble while I've been asleep?' he asked.

'Nothing so far. I reckon if that *hombre* is still on our tail he's either decided to hole up for a while or he's some miles away. If he'd found the canyon by now, I figure he'd have made his way through it before nightfall. That trail is likely to be treacherous in the dark. A man could slip and go over the side if he didn't look where he was puttin' his feet.'

'I'll feel a lot safer as far as he's

concerned, once I know exactly where he is,' Clint muttered. He went over to the door and stepped outside, feeling the coolness of the night air, flowing down from the higher ridges, on his face. The sleep had refreshed him. Now he could feel the strength returning to his body and his brain was clearer than before. Overhead, the sky was ablaze with a multitude of stars right down to the very horizons. There was a faint yellow glow in the east indicating the presence of moon-rise.

Merriam drew in a deep breath and then let it fall. His smile was a little pinched out and Clint looked at him sharply, surprised by the change in the other.

'I sure hope you're not goin' to worry overmuch about this *hombre*. If he don't put in an appearance after tomorrow, he never will. I know this kind of country. There's nothing but bare rock and dust out yonder, not a drop of water to be had for miles. On foot a man doesn't stand a chance in hell of staying alive for more'n a couple of days and by the end of the first day and night, he's so goshdarned tuckered out from lack of sleep and thirst, he won't be able to think straight. I figure he made a bad mistake back at the plateau when he slipped off into the rocks without botherin' to take the horse. If he'd been thinking straight then he'd have taken a horse and all of our supplies with him. That way, we'd have been finished.'

The other swung away from him, heading back into the shack with confidence. 'I reckon I'll get myself some sleep,' he called from the interior of the shack. 'You goin' to keep watch all night?'

'I reckon so,' Clint said softly. He reached out for the Winchester, went outside to check the horses. It was as he reached them that the thought came to him anew that they still hadn't seen anything of the horse that Calton had been riding. It must have been somewhere in these hills and if the gunhawk managed to lay his hands on it —

He let his thoughts wander on, striking a match and lighting a cigarette, pulling the smoke down into his lungs. He had the inescapable feeling that things were happening about which he knew nothing, and the feeling troubled him. Going back to the shack, he sat down on the wooden step and stared moodily out into the night, watching as the moon lifted from the horizon and sailed majestically into the clear sky, throwing its yellow radiance over everything. The clearing stood out brilliantly in that glaring light and the canyon trail was thrown into deep shadow in which nothing seemed to move.

It was a little after midnight when he heard the faint sound in the distance. For a moment, the sound seemed so distorted by the echoes which were reflected from it that he could not make out with certainty what it was. Then he recognized the distant break of gunfire. It came from many miles away, but he felt a quiver of apprehension run through him at the sound. The only one they knew to be out there was the outlaw they had brought with them and who had slipped away at the first opportunity. But that gunfire had come from several guns, indicating a large party somewhere in the territory.

7

Showdown!

The gunfire carried far over the rocks, echoing along the canyon which acted as a natural funnel for it, strangely magnifying the sound. Clint came to his feet swiftly, still gripping the rifle, straining his ears as he tried to pick out the direction from which it came, but there were so many criss-crossing echoes breaking from the main source of the sound that it was impossible to do so and eventually he gave it up and concentrated on trying to figure out how many men there were.

At the first sound, he heard the movement behind him in the shack and a moment later, Merriam appeared in the doorway at his back, blinking his eyes against the flooding moonlight, his face hard and tense.

'That's quite a ways off and well into the hills back towards the main trail if I'm any judge,' he said finally. He rubbed the beard on his chin with a faint scratching sound. 'What do you figure it is, Clint?'

'Hard to say. I didn't notice any dust cloud along the trail behind us during the two days we were headed in this direction. But it's just possible that we were followed. I reckon we were much too busy worryin' about that *hombre* who tried to sneak up on us to bother about any party that might be followin' us at a distance.'

'You figure it may be Jess Durman and his crew?'

'That's possible. If they rode back into town and had a word with the sheriff, they may have guessed which way we were headed and Durman knows these trails like the back of his hand.'

'Then why in tarnation are they shootin' yonder, givin' themselves away?'

Clint tightened his lips. There could be only one possible explanation, he reckoned. Somehow, they had bumped into that man who had been trailing Merriam and himself and a gunfight had broken out.

'Sounds like quite a gun battle,' he said after a moment. 'Must be that *hombre* who was tailin' us. He's probably bumped into Durman and his boys and decided to shoot it out. Hear those rifles blastin'? Hard to make out how many there are with those echoes bouncing about like that.'

'Must be Durman and his crew,' said the other after a brief, reflective pause. 'Can't think of anythin' else it might be.'

Clint's eyes narrowed as he turned to glance at the other. 'Might not be Durman at all,' he opined, though he didn't really believe this deep down. He knew those shots must be coming from about the place where the main trail led past the Indian's Head Rocks and up into the hills. If that was the case, it served to indicate that the outlaw had not been trailing them deeper into the hills but had decided to try to head back towards the trail. Maybe he had figured that without water, he didn't stand any chance of survival at all and he already knew enough to enable him to ride back and stand a good chance of locating the El Dorado Mine again.

'If that is Durman, then the odds are that he'll bring his men up here to look for us.' Merriam said sharply. He threw an alert glance in the direction of the horses. 'I figure we'd better get the mounts out of sight.'

They untethered the mounts and led them across the smooth ground to the mine entrance, herded them inside, tethering them a few yards back where they could not be seen from outside. The horses did not like it there and pranced angrily before they were finally brought under control.

Going back to the shack, Clint rummaged around among the boxes at the rear of the small building. Merriam eyed him in surprise. Then he said: 'If you're lookin' for more ammunition or weapons, I reckon you're outa luck. There'll be nothin' like that in there. Whoever was here would take guns with them when they pulled out.'

'I'm not lookin' for guns. I figured there might be some dynamite still around and it's probably our only chance if Durman has got a large bunch of men with him.'

He saw the gust of expression that went over the other's face, then the old prospector gave a swift nod. 'You're right. There should be some of the stuff still lyin' around. If we can't find any of that, they may have left some gunpowder and fuse behind. You figurin' on blockin' the canyon pass with it?'

'Somethin' like that,' Clint said through his teeth. He began pulling the old rags away which had been used to cover the multitude of wooden boxes stacked high against the rear wall of the cabin. 'We've got to be careful though. We don't want to start an avalanche that will block the canyon completely, otherwise we might not be able to get out ourselves.'

The first few boxes they examined were empty although it was obvious that they had originally contained sticks of dynamite. Clint felt a sinking feeling in his chest. If they had to face up to Durman and his crew of hired killers with only the guns they had, their chances of holding them off for any length of time were pretty remote, in spite of the obvious fact that the canyon favoured defence rather than attack. Two men could hold off an army of attackers, it was true, but only so long as the ammunition or supplies lasted. After that, they were finished and Durman would know that. But with high explosive it might be possible to lay a trap for the others and destroy most of Durman's force in one single blow.

Merriam moved away and came back a moment later with a lantern. Striking a match, he lit the lamp, replaced the glass cover, brought it over to the back of the cabin and held it up as Clint searched.

'Hell, it looks as though we're plumb out of luck,' Clint said through his clenched teeth. 'Nothin' here at all.' He threw the rags back over the empty boxes, the lids of which had all been prised loose some time before and their contents removed.

'Somethin' yonder in the corner,' Merriam lifted the lantern higher so that the light penetrated into the gloom picking out the two barrels set into the corner of the shack.

Going forward, Clint bent, placed his arms around one and lifted, gave a sharp gasp of satisfaction as he felt the weight of it drag on his shoulder muscles. He tried to heave the other on to its side and finally succeeded in doing so, going down on one knee to examine it more closely, spilling a few of the black grains into the palm of his hand. Then he nodded slowly.

'Gunpowder,' he said quietly. 'There's

enough here for what I've got in mind. Now we'd better scout around for some fuse.'

They found it a few moments later, tucked away behind one of the boxes. Clint took out a long coil of it, examined it closely. 'You ever handled this stuff before?' he asked the other.

'Nope,' Merriam shook his head. 'Seen what it can do, but that's about all.'

Carefully, Clint cut a length from the fuse about three feet long. He gestured towards the large watch the other displayed proudly in his pocket. 'That timepiece any good,' he asked.

'Sure it is,' nodded the other. He pulled it out, held it to his ear, shaking it a little.

'Hand it over,' Clint held out his hand. 'I'll have to time this fuse. 'We've got to judge the length of fuse to make sure the gunpowder will go off at the right moment.'

He carried the fuse outside the shack, stretched it out on the ground, then struck a match and applied it to one end. There was a bright streak of flame that came jetting from the end of the fuse as it began to burn slowly along its snaking length. By burning three pieces of the same length, Clint was able to ascertain the speed at which it burned. Satisfied, he handed the watch back to the old prospector.

Glancing up at the bright, moonlit sky, he said softly. 'I figure that Durman and his boys won't reach the canyon until around dawn. We've still got three or four hours to set up the trap for 'em.'

Carrying one barrel of the gunpowder each, they made their way across the smooth clearing to the yawning black mouth of the canyon. Clint threw a swift glance up at the towering rocks that loomed over their heads, caught sight of the narrow trail that led up them. It was steep and strewn with boulders and sharp rocks, but it was the only way up.

'Think you can make it, old-timer?' he asked solicitously.

The other snorted. 'Sure I can make it,' he retorted. 'Just lead the way and save your breath for the climbin'.'

Turning, smiling a little to himself at the other's righteous indignation, Clint began to climb. Feet slipping on the treacherous ground, clawing himself up with one hand, the other gripping the barrel of gunpowder tightly where it rested on his shoulder, he worked his way up among the rocks, searching carefully in the moonlight for any obstacles in his path. Several times, he was forced to pause for breath and long before he had reached the top of the narrow trail, the strain of the climb was beginning to tell on him. His leg and shoulder muscles ached like fire and the barrel of gunpowder weighed a ton. How Merriam was faring he did not know. He could hear the other's boots scraping on the rock as he pulled himself up after him, but it was impossible on that narrow trail to turn and look behind him. All he could do was keep on moving and trust that the older man had sufficient strength and endurance to keep him moving.

After what seemed an eternity, he moved out into a patch of moonlight and saw to his relief that the trail was no longer ascending, but ran on level in front of him. Here, too, it was a little wider, and there were fewer rocks to impede his progress. He moved forward a couple of yards, sucking air down into his lungs, and then squatted with his back against the rocks on one side of the trail, legs thrust out in front of him, the barrel of gunpowder set down beside him, and waited for Merriam to come up.

At last, the other's head appeared and he thrust himself over the lip of the trail with one last, almost despairing heave of his legs, lowering the barrel in front of him, the breath wheezing in and out of his throat. He wiped the back of his hand over his sweat-covered, dust-smeared features.

'You all right?' Clint asked.

'Sure, sure.' Somehow, the other got

the words out, sank back on to his haunches. 'How much further do we have to go?'

'We're on the top of the trail right now,' Clint told him. 'We'll move on for a few hundred feet until we get to a spot where the rocks overlook the trail down yonder. We've got to ensure that when the explosive goes off it will send part of the ledge down on to the trail.'

'You figurin' on buryin' half of 'em under an avalanche?'

The other chewed thoughtfully on his lower lip, nodding in agreement.

'That's the general idea. We've got to lay the fuse and light it so as to give us chance to get away when the explosive goes off and yet it will have to go off at just the right moment to catch the party when they ride underneath. I'm bankin' on 'em takin' their time through the canyon. They'll be expectin' trouble and they'll be wary.'

'Could be they'll all be riding in single file and that won't make it easy to catch many of 'em under the rocks,' put in Merriam.

'That's why we'll put the two barrels of gunpowder some distance away from each other. That way, we should be able to trap most of 'em.'

They rested for five minutes, and then struggled to their feet again. In the moonlight, there were too many shadows along the trail and as he edged his way forward, Clint realized how easy it would be to put a foot wrong and go tumbling down the sheer side of the ledge on to the rocky canyon floor a couple of hundred feet below. He could hear the other edging forward behind him, could pick out the sharp gale of the older man's breathing, knew the strain with which he was forcing himself to move, carrying that heavy barrel of powder.

At last, Clint stopped, waited for Merriam to come up to him. 'Put your barrel down here,' he said sharply. 'I'll take this one on another hundred yards or so. That ought to give us enough leeway to trap most of them.'

There was a taut grimness in his mind as he edged further along the trail. It seemed to be narrowing swiftly now and in places he was forced to stand absolutely still with his back and shoulders pressed hard against the solid unyielding rock behind him, with his feet almost over the rough edge of the trail, knowing that one wrong move, even to the extent of bending his legs, would send him pitching forward away from the rock and down into that abyss of blackness that yawned at his feet. He sucked air into his lungs, acutely aware of the chill coldness of the sweat that had broken out on his body, running in irritating little rivulets down his face, getting into his eyes and tasting saltily on his lips. An inch at a time, he edged his way sideways. A loose rock crumbled away from the lip of the trail as his foot rested momentarily on it and went bounding down the slope, crashing loudly in the darkness as it fell.

The sweat broke out anew on the small of his back and he held his breath for so long that it hurt in his lungs. There was a little tremor in his legs that threatened to overwhelm him, to send him staggering forward away from the strangely reassuring hardness of the rocky face at his back. Shuffling his feet one at a time, he finally succeeded in edging his way past the loose break in the trail. He continued in this way for another fifty yards before he finally paused, lowered the heavy barrel from his shoulders and went down on one knee, searching the rocks here for a safe place in which to set the gunpowder. At last he located the narrow shelf of rock perhaps two feet wide that jutted out from the main rock wall at this point. Gently, he set the barrel down on it, wedged it carefully in place with large rocks, then knocked a small hole into the lid of the barrel, inserting the end of the coil of fuse into it. This done, he piled more stones and rocks around it, then pushed himself to his feet and began to edge back along the way he had come.

If anything, the return journey was more difficult than before. True he no longer had to carry the weight of the gunpowder, but now he had to back away, trailing the length of fuse out in front of him, making sure that it did not fall too close to the lip of the ledge where it could either be dragged over the side by its own weight, or possibly be spotted by some sharp-eyed gunman riding the trail below.

Reaching the point along the ledge where he had almost fallen before, he tested it for footing, paused for a moment thinking of the tremendous depth below, then sucked in a sharp gust of air and moved back.

'You all right, Clint?' Merriam's voice reached him from the moonlit trail.

'Sure,' he called back. There was a sharp edge of tension to his tone though in spite of the tight rein he had damped on his emotions. 'There's a rough bit of trail here only about two feet wide.'

The other made no reply to that. Very

slowly, Clint navigated the stretch of trail, then moved along more quickly to where Merriam still crouched with his back to the rock face.

'There, I figure that ought to do it for that barrel,' he said softly. 'Now we'll get this one in place and run the fuse back yonder.' He jerked a thumb in the direction of a bend in the ledge. 'We don't want to be in plain view of those men when we have to light the fuses.'

Merriam gave a quick nod. 'You figurin' on stayin' the rest of the night up here on the ledge?'

'Can you think of anythin' better?'

'Guess not.' The other shifted his position a little to give Clint more room in which to work. Now came the moment when he was glad he had taken the trouble to check the burning speed of this fuse. Mentally, he estimated how long it would take that length which he had led to the first barrel to burn and then cut off a length of fuse which he rammed into the second barrel, arranging it so that the first would go off a few seconds ahead of the other. His aim was to start a couple of miniature landslides here, trapping as many men as possible down on the trail. He had no way of telling how many men Durman would have with him when he arrived, in fact they were not sure that it was Durman back there who had started that shooting. But they could not afford to take any chances now. One thing was certain. Whoever it was, they were interested in the location of the El Dorado Mine. There could be no other explanation for why they would be following that trail.

Once everything was in position and the two ends of the fuse had been set along the trail, pinned into position by a couple of rocks, Clint sank back on to his haunches, leaned his shoulders against the rocks, and forced his heart into a slower, more normal beat. That long climb and the moving up and down that narrow ledge with danger a constant companion, waiting for the slightest slip, had taken its toll of him.

They settled down to wait for the coming of the dawn and with it. the anticipated arrival of Jess Durman and his crew.

★　★　★

Not more than an hour earlier, Durman had led his party off the main trail, swinging up into the rocky country that lay to the north. It had been a simple matter to follow the tracks of Lanner and the man he had with him. He had ridden into town a day after Lanner had pulled out with that old prospector and it had not taken him long to discover where the two of them were headed. He himself, was not sure whether he believed in this old silver mine that was reputed to contain the richest seam ever discovered, but if the trail would lead him to Lanner, then he intended to follow it to its bitter end.

They had sighted that curious rock formation shortly before sundown the previous evening and had cut up into the rocks without pause. Some of the men had argued against riding along that trail during the night, pointing out that it would be easy for them to be trapped and shot down from cover, but he had forced them on, arguing that they were following only two men and they outnumbered the others by more than fifteen to one.

Darkness caught them at the camp which Clint and Merriam had made the previous night but they had not paused, had merely examined the trail there before riding on into the darkening hills.

'Don't you reckon we're headed for trouble, boss?' muttered Lawson, the new foreman. 'They could have turned off the trail some way back. They did that once before, remember?'

'I ain't forgettin' that,' Durman said sharply. 'But there's no place here where they could break off. Besides, I doubt if they know we're followin' them. Come ahead. We may be able to take 'em by surprise and they can lead us to this mine if there is such a place.'

'I reckon there has to be,' went on the other tightly. 'They wouldn't come into this wilderness unless they were fairly sure there was somethin' here for 'em.' A look of greed crossed his bluff features and it was not lost on Durman.

The rancher said tersely. 'Just keep your mind on your work, Lawson. I brung you and the boys out here to hunt down this *hombre*, Lanner. When he's dead, then we can start lookin' for this lost mine. If there is such a place and we find anythin', that's the time to start worryin' about silver.'

'Won't be too easy to follow 'em ahead,' broke in one of the other men, pointing. 'When they worked here they must've used burros. A horse can't travel through this country without runnin' the risk of breakin' a leg. You get halfway along this trail and if you encounter a break then you're finished. You won't be able to turn.'

'We go on ahead,' snapped Durman. 'And I'll hear no more of turnin' back or campin' for the night. I mean to keep on their trail until I catch up with them. Get that?'

'I've seen country like this in daylight and I say it can't be done,' argued the other hoarsely. He gripped the reins of his mount tightly in both hands, facing the rancher. 'If you ask me there's only this one trail up into the hills and they can't get out of this wilderness without gettin' past us. We've got plenty of time to run 'em to earth.'

'They can't be too far ahead of us,' said Durman impatiently.

'Then they'll still be there in the mornin' and we'll be able to see what we're doin'. It's sheer suicide to move up there in the darkness.'

'Hell, there's moonlight,' snapped the rancher tautly. 'We've got more'n enough light to see by.' He turned savagely in his saddle, waved his right hand. 'All right,' he called. 'Let's move. Keep your eyes open and if you see anythin' that moves, shoot to kill. Remember, I want this *hombre* Lanner dead.'

The men grumbled, but they followed on, gigging their mounts as the horses slowed, pawing at the ground, not wanting to move forward into this treacherous country.

They rode over the rough ledge of the plateau and then cut out into the rocks and it was less than two minutes later that the shot rang out from the cover of one of the boulders and the man riding beside Jess Durman pitched forward in his saddle, arched up for a moment as he strove to stay upright, then toppled to one side. One leg caught in the stirrup and the frightened animal, spooked by the sudden, unexpected sound, reared up then ran on along the twisting, rocky trail, dragging the man along with it, hauling his body over the rough ground.

Savagely, cursing loudly, Durman pulled his mount back from the trail, into the shadowed rocks to one side, while the rest of the men scattered, firing into the boulders. Their first shots merely ricocheted and whined off the rock, but one bullet found its mark in yielding flesh and Durman caught a glimpse of the man who suddenly broke cover and began to move away into the rocks away from the trail, head and shoulders kept low to present a more difficult target. He pulled himself round quickly, gave a savage snarl and lifted his Colt, resting the barrel on his arm as he sighted it on the running figure and pulled the trigger twice in rapid succession. The sound of the shots boomed in his ears and in the flooding moonlight he saw, with a sense of satisfaction, the running figure suddenly stop, rear up on to its toes, and then crash over the ledge and fall several feet on to the trail. Once the shooting had died, he remained where he was while the slowly strophying echoes ran off into the distance. When there was no further gunfire, he pulled out from the shadows and walked his mount along the trail towards the crumpled body lying near the rocks.

Slipping from the saddle, he went

down on one knee and rolled the man over. He felt a sudden sense of defeat as he stared into the features of the dead man.

Lawson came forward, looked down. 'Reckon that was a fool thing for him to do,' he said shortly. 'Openin' fire on us like that. If he'd stayed where he was and kept quiet, we'd have ridden on past him without knowin' he was there. Any idea who it is?'

'Never seen him before in my life,' Durman straightened up, shook his head. 'It sure ain't Lanner. I figured it might have been him.'

'Then he's still somewhere in there.' The other threw an arm towards the towering rocks which lay ahead of them, black shadows strewn among them in the glancing moonlight.

'What happened to Harry?'

'Dead,' said the other tonelessly. 'Bullet got him in the chest. He was dead before he fell out of the saddle.'

'All right. Get mounted up again. We're moving on and let that be a lesson to everybody. Lanner is no fool and he may have spotted us and be lyin' in wait for us in the hills. If that's the case, then we can expect trouble at any minute.'

They rode slowly now, keeping in single file where the trail narrowed and it was almost grey dawn with the moon and stars paling in the east before they moved out of the flat country and came in sight of the canyon that stretched away in front of them, rocky walls rising sheer up into the sky.

Durman reined his mount and sat for a long moment in the saddle, studying the lie of the land which lay ahead of them, troubled more than he cared to admit. If there was any plan for an attack being made against them then this was the logical place for it. He cast about him for a long moment but it was soon apparent that there was no other way into the hills. To scout around and try to find some other trail that might lead them through would take the best part of a day or so and might even then end in failure.

Lifting himself in the saddle, he motioned the men forward, passing between the sky-rearing walls of rock which lifted sheer on either side, closing in on them as they rode deeper into the canyon. As he rode, he kept turning his head, running his gaze from side to side, watching for the first sign of trouble.

★   ★   ★

'There they are,' Clint said suddenly. He pushed himself up on to his knees, pointed along the trail, far off into the distance. From their vantage point, it was just possible for them to make out the group of riders as they snaked in single file through the canyon. As he had expected, the others had caught up with them shortly before dawn.

Merriam moved his body slightly, narrowing his eyes as he glanced in the direction of the approaching column.

'Can you make out who it is?' he queried.

Clint shook his head. 'Too far away,' he muttered thinly. 'But I'm bettin' it's Durman and his crew.'

'Reckon they'll spot us up here?' asked the other. 'They'll be wary and expectin' trouble.'

'By the time they ride down that stretch of the trail, it'll be too late for any of 'em to do anythin' about it,' Clint said tautly. He checked the two lengths of fuse that snaked back among the rocks to where the barrels of gunpowder were stacked. In his mind's eye, he could visualize what the outcome would be once they exploded, could imagine the thousands of tons of rock and boulders that would go rumbling down the steep side of the trail, falling on to the men riding below, giving them no chance whatever of getting out from under that crushing weight of rock. For a moment, the full enormity of what he was about to do penetrated his mind, but he shook the feeling away. Those men riding with Jess Durman were all hardened killers, would shoot down Merriam and himself without a second thought, as if they were animals.

Then he thought of Everett, dying on that lonesome trail far to the north, a frightened man, hounded by this pack of killers — for now he felt sure that it was some of Durman's men who had eventually caught up with the other and tried to get their hands on that map. What gave him this sudden feeling of conviction he did not know but it strengthened his resolve to go through with this.

Motioning the other back behind the bend in the ledge, he stretched himself out on the rocky outcrop of ground, placed the box of matches close beside him, then settled himself to wait with a stony patience.

The column seemed to come on at a snail's pace but now, he could make out the man in the lead as the grey light of dawn began to filter down from the brightning sky and he saw that it was, indeed, Jess Durman, leading his men on through the canyon. Tightening his lips grimly, he watched as they rode forward, their horses picking their way slowly over the upthrusting boulders which littered the trail. They were clearly wary, kept staring up at the ledges which ran along the rocky face above the trail. Clint felt a little tremor go through him and it seemed that Durman looked directly at him, shading his eyes a little as he peered along the side of the trail. In another three minutes they would be almost directly below the point where the first barrel of gunpowder had been placed, he reckoned. He reached out for the box of matches, struck one after gauging the time it would take for that fuse to burn along its whole length. He wanted Durman and most of the men well past that point before it exploded. He hesitated a moment, aware of what the result of his action would be. He knew that Durman would remain stubbornly on that trail, would follow him to the bitter end, was determined to finish him no matter what the cost.

Striking the match, he applied the flame to the end of the fuse, saw the spurt of orange flame that came from them, then wriggled back along the trail taking care not to show himself over the edge.

A moment later, he was beside Merriam. The other eyed him briefly for a moment and in a voice that was little more than a whisper, Clint said. 'Both fuses are lit now. We ought to be far enough away just here to be out of danger.' He knew that most of the blast would be directed downward reflected from the solid rock wall at one side of the trail.

They waited tensely as the seconds ticked by. It was possible now, in the deep and clinging silence to make out the sound of hoofbeats on the canyon floor down below yet they dared not lean forward to see where the others were for fear of being spotted. A minute went by, then another. Had the fuse failed? Clint found himself wondering as the seconds lengthened. It had been kept back in that shack for God knew how long, might even be damp and useless. The barrels in which the gunpowder had been kept had seemed sound and dry even after all that time and in any case —

His thoughts gelled in his head as the first barrel of gunpowder went off with a cavernous roar that set his teeth on edge. The deep rumbling echoes were thrown back at them from the opposite side of the canyon and scarcely had the sounds hammered at their eardrums, half deafening them, than the second barrel went off and close on the heels of the savage roar came the deeper-toned sound of thousands of tons of rocks and boulders pitching away from the sides of the canyon and rolling down in a growing avalanche on to the riders clustered below. With an effort, Clint forced himself to move. Through the haze of dust, he glanced down below, could just make out the mass of rock which had gone bouncing down the side of the canyon. Plummeting and crashing, it was as if the entire side of the mountain had suddenly come away over a hundred-yard stretch, burying everything on the trail below. Deafened by the thunder, choking on the dust that lifted high into the air, Clint struggled to see through the haze. At first, he could make out nothing, then he saw with a fascinated horror that almost the whole of the column had vanished, completely obliterated under that river of rock and stone which had roared down on them without warning.

'Let's get down there,' Clint said hoarsely. He wiped his face with the sleeve of his jacket.

Twenty minutes later, they made their way forward along the narrow trail to the area of destruction. He had his gun in his hand and ducked sharply as a shot rang out from the side of the canyon.

'God damn you, Lanner,' yelled a voice that he recognized instantly. 'I figured it was you who did that. But this is the end of the trail for you.'

Swivelling on his heels, Clint swung in the direction of the other's voice, saw Durman standing with his back to the rocky wall, the gun in his right hand already lifting to cover him and fire the killing shot. Plain instinct made him swing to one side and so miss the bullet that the other flung at him. The gun in his hand roared as he pressed the trigger. Even as he hit the ground, he triggered again, saw Durman stand for a moment with that look of incredulous astonishment written all over his big face. Then he dropped forward into the dust to lie still.

Going forward slowly, Clint turned him over, then gave Merriam a quick nod as the other came running up. 'He's dead,' he said dully, and felt momentarily surprised that he did not feel such a sense of triumph as he had expected.

'Where are the others?' Merriam asked. He cast about him cautiously.

'I figure they must've decided to head back now that most of the party was killed.' Clint said slowly. 'I doubt if we'll have any more trouble from them. Durman is dead and the men who rode with him have either been killed or they'll be headin' out along the trail over the hills. Anywhere so long as they get away from here.'

Wearily, he thrust the gun back into its holster, turned away from the scene of utter destruction. The trail had not been completely blocked by the avalanche and there was still a narrow passage through.

★　★　★

A week later, after the claim to the El Dorado Mine had been registered in their names, Clint and Merriam sat their mounts once again at the fork in the trails out of town.

'You sure you know what you're

doin'?' asked the other, eyeing him sharply from beneath bushy brows. 'You'll be headin' back in this direction soon?'

'Try to keep me away,' Clint said, grinning. 'Just you go ahead and start diggin' that silver out of the El Dorado. I've just got a little unfinished business to attend to at a little ranch up north, a couple of days' ride.'

The other gave a quick nod. His lips widened in a grin. 'I hope for your sake she says yes,' he said knowingly. 'Can't see how she'll refuse though when she knows how much silver you've got.'

Wheeling his mount, Merriam swung away down the main street of the town, heading back south, back to the hills that lay beyond the Indian's Head Rocks. Clint watched him for a moment, then swung the head of his horse north. He had promised he would ride back to the Winton ranch and this was one promise he really intended to keep.

BRAZOS STATION

Clayton Nash

Caleb Brett liked his job as deputy sheriff and being betrothed to the sheriff's daughter, Rose. What he didn't like was the thought of the sheriff moving in with them once they were married. But capturing the infamous outlaw Gil Bannerman offered a way out because there was plenty of reward money. Then came Brett's big mistake — he lost Bannerman and was framed. Now everything he treasured was lost. Did he have a chance in hell of fighting his way back?

DEAD IS FOR EVER

Amy Sadler

After rescuing Hope Bennett from the clutches of two trailbums, Sam Carver made a serious mistake. He killed one of the outlaws, and reckoned on collecting the bounty on Lew Daggett. But catching Sam off-guard, Daggett made off with the girl, leaving Sam for dead. However, he was only grazed and once he came to, he set out in search of Hope. When he eventually found her, he was forced into a dramatic showdown with his life on the line.

SMOKING STAR

B. J. Holmes

In the one-horse town of Medicine Bluff two men were dead. Sheriff Jack Starr didn't need the badge on his chest to spur him into tracking the killer. He had his own reason for seeking justice, a reason no-one knew. It drove him to take a journey into the past where he was to discover something else that was to add even greater urgency to the situation — to stop Montana's rivers running red with blood.

THE WIND WAGON

Troy Howard

Sheriff Al Corning was as tough as they came and with his four seasoned deputies he kept the peace in Laramie — at least until the squatters came. To fend off starvation, the settlers took some cattle off the cowmen, including Jonas Lefler. A hard, unforgiving man, Lefler retaliated with lynchings. Things got worse when one of the squatters revealed he was a former Texas lawman — and no mean shooter. Could Sheriff Corning prevent further bloodshed?

CABEL

Paul K. McAfee

Josh Cabel returned home from the Civil War to find his family all murdered by rioting members of Quantrill's band. The hunt for the killers led Josh to Colorado City where, after months of searching, he finally settled down to work on a ranch nearby. He saved the life of an Indian, who led him to a cache of weapons waiting for Sitting Bull's attack on the Whites. His involvement threw Cabel into grave danger. When the final confrontation came, who had the fastest — and deadlier — draw?

RIVERBOAT

Alan C. Porter

When Rufus Blake died he was found to be carrying a gold bar from a Confederate gold shipment that had disappeared twenty years before. This inspires Wes Hardiman and Ben Travis to swap horse and trail for a riverboat, the *River Queen*, on the Mississippi, in an effort to find the missing gold. Cord Duval is set on destroying the *River Queen* and he has the power and the gunmen to do it. Guns blaze as Hardiman and Travis attempt to unravel the mystery and stay alive.